Prologue

I was birthed on a cold December morning in the San Francisco Peaks, birthed of a woman whose name I wasn't told. She was a camp follower, I guess, which is a whole lot more of a civilized thing to call your mama than a whore. Which my daddy always did. Daddy hadn't much time for females except for the relieving of manly urges, and I guess he was fit to be tied when she turned up on his stoop that fall, big as a house with me.

I will credit my daddy with taking her in, though. He couldn't even be sure I was his, could he? He said he told her she could stay there in his cabin and stay warm until the baby came, but come spring he was off to the silver fields of Colorado and he was going alone, no two ways about it.

Anyhow, that's what he said. Well, my mama

up and died giving me life, and he was plain stuck with me, I guess. It couldn't have been easy for a big, tough old bird like him to cart around a baby and fix bottles and change nappies, but he did it. Frankly, I'm surprised he didn't just give me to some nice family he come across in his travels.

But no, he kept me around and pretty well fed by breaking rock all over Colorado, then California, and finally back to Arizona, to the southern town of Tombstone.

I was fifteen by then and there was no question he was my daddy, for I was his spitting image. He said he guessed I'd better start bringing home some of the bacon if I wanted to stay there. "There" was a miner's shack, although I think *"shack"* was probably too grand a word for it. Daddy was six feet, three and one half inches tall, and he couldn't lie down without opening the door. On cold nights, he had to choose which to freeze—his head or his toes.

I was coming up to his size already. All angles and elbows and high-water pants, that was me. Of course, when you're in a mining camp and it's just fellers around, you don't mind a thing like that so much. But when you live right outside a regular metropolis—like Tombstone was in those days—and there are girls about to whisper and giggle behind their gloves, it is a whole different matter.

THE
BROTHERS OF
JUNIOR DOYLE

E. K. Recknor

A SIGNET BOOK

SIGNET
Published by New American Library, a division of
Penguin Group (USA) Inc., 375 Hudson Street,
New York, New York 10014, USA
Penguin Group (Canada), 90 Eglinton Avenue East, Suite 700, Toronto,
Ontario M4P 2Y3, Canada (a division of Pearson Penguin Canada Inc.)
Penguin Books Ltd., 80 Strand, London WC2R 0RL, England
Penguin Ireland, 25 St. Stephen's Green, Dublin 2,
Ireland (a division of Penguin Books Ltd.)
Penguin Group (Australia), 250 Camberwell Road, Camberwell, Victoria 3124,
Australia (a division of Pearson Australia Group Pty. Ltd.)
Penguin Books India Pvt. Ltd., 11 Community Centre, Panchsheel Park,
New Delhi - 110 017, India
Penguin Group (NZ), 67 Apollo Drive, Mairangi Bay,
Auckland 1311, New Zealand (a division of Pearson New Zealand Ltd.)
Penguin Books (South Africa) (Pty.) Ltd., 24 Sturdee Avenue,
Rosebank, Johannesburg 2196, South Africa

Penguin Books Ltd., Registered Offices:
80 Strand, London WC2R 0RL, England

First published by Signet, an imprint of New American Library,
a division of Penguin Group (USA) Inc.

First Printing, May 2007
10 9 8 7 6 5 4 3 2 1

Anyhow, I didn't find out about Daddy's other pups until later on. And even then, I can't say I was real thrilled with most of them, except at the first. It ain't nice or romantic or any of that stuff to have a brother who would have got himself hanged except they judged him as crazy as a loony bird. Especially one that almost took you with him.

1

Daddy and me worked at the old Three Strikes Mining Enterprise just outside Tombstone with a lot of others, and she was putting out some good metal, mostly silver. Daddy went down the shaft every day except for Sundays, but he got me a job taking care of the horses and mules that carted out what rock they dug and blasted each day, and turned the *arristra*.

I won't say it was the nicest job, what with having to listen to Old Man Thorogood bitch and moan all the time about how his miners were robbing him blind, or how I was shorting his animals on feed, or how the French Mexicans were sneaking in at night—to do what, I had no idea—but I guess there could have been worse ways to make a living.

Still, I didn't much cotton to going to work

every day. Didn't like the routine, I guess, always doing the same old things, always smelling like mule shit. Didn't much like taking orders from Old Man Thorogood, either. Most especially, I didn't like to see Daddy taking orders from him.

Why, if he'd been of a mind, my daddy could have tied Thorogood up in knots, like a German pretzel!

But Daddy didn't. He was a good man.

I guess maybe I wasn't so good. Maybe that was my mama's side coming out in me, or at least I imagined it was. The hunger for the wild things, I mean, and the wild places. And wanting some mischief to get up to.

I don't mean the usual kind of mischief, like tipping cows or upturning somebody's outhouse. I mean the more serious kind. I had a great admiration, in those days, for Doc Holliday and his ilk. I wanted to do grand things, like play cards and be a good shot and have books writ about me, and have people say my name in a hushed tone.

But before I get into it, I suppose I ought to tell you my name. I was born Patrick (more often called Paddy) Doyle, Jr., after my dad—which shows a lot of faith on his part, if you ask me, seeing as how he didn't really know for certain he was my daddy at the time he named me.

I've got his blue eyes. Not that blue eyes were uncommon. Lots of people have them. But except for Daddy, they didn't have my kind. They're real pale, icy blue, a light turquoise, sort of, and rimmed with black, which I'm told makes a striking impression on folks, ladies included, when coupled with my black hair. And I don't mean dark brown. I mean black. In the sunlight, it was practically blue.

Anyway.

When I was sixteen, Daddy got shot. I didn't see it, which I suppose is just as well. When I came off shift from the stables, I heard a couple of far-off rifle shots—probably somebody out after jackrabbits or partridge, I thought—and then I saw a bunch of rock-breakers gathered down by the main shaft. Being the curious sort, I went down to see what was going on.

When I got there, though, there came Old Man Thorogood, popping out of the crowd real nervous-like and trying to move me away. 'Course, I was about a foot taller than he was—and kind of mad at him anyway, on account of he'd put down one of my favorite mules that morning, just because she had the heaves—so I shoved my way past him and elbowed the crowd aside.

I stopped quick. There at my feet sprawled Daddy, like he'd just lay down to take him a nap, save for the little round hole centering his

forehead and the spreading pool of blood looking like a big flat red pillow. I don't much recall
what happened next, not until I found myself
back at the main shack, seated on a barrel and
hearing Butch Tanner, the shift boss, and Old
Man Thorogood discussing my future.

"We could keep him on," Butch said, just like
I wasn't there. "He's sure big enough. He could
take Big Paddy's place on the drill crew."

"No," Thorogood muttered, scratching his
chin. "I want to keep him with the livestock.
He's good with 'em. He's the only one around
here that can handle Katarina and Hector." They
were two of my favorite mules, along with
Spice, the one he'd put down.

They thought I was still nonsensical, and so
they were pretty surprised when all of a sudden
I said, "No."

"Now, son . . ." began Thorogood, but I cut
him short.

"Why ain't you out looking for the man who
shot Daddy?" I demanded, my hands balling
into fists. "Why would anyone . . . Why?"

And then I started bawling, just like a kid. I
hated like hell for them to see that, but I
couldn't help myself.

To make a long story short, they didn't look
at all for Daddy's killer, and I ran away from
home, such as it was, and straight into the arms
of an older woman. That was Ruby Tulayne, a

grown woman of twenty-eight years who had a little crib on the edge of town, out by the tent city. I had met her a couple of times before, when Daddy sent me into town for supplies.

I didn't get to spend too much time with her—I always had to find something to do between seven in the evening and four in the morning, since she was busy earning a living—but it was Ruby Tulayne what started teaching me how to read and write as good as I do. Daddy had taught me my numbers, but that was all he knew to teach.

My daddy had come over from County Cork back in the old days, when he was just a lad of six. His mama and daddy died of sickness there in New York City within a year, and he was on his own. He was too busy working (and stealing, I suppose) to go to school, so don't go thinking that he was stupid or anything. He was just sort of preoccupied with staying alive.

Anyhow, it was while I was living in town with Ruby Tulayne that I met Doc Holliday for real. Oh, I'd seen him before lots of times, but he was always busy with cards or conversation or drink. Mostly drink. But this time, while I was killing time waiting for Ruby to be done working, I was walking up Allen Street and ran smack into him.

At first, I was terrible scared. People said Doc would kill you for saying "boo" to him, and I guess that was one of the things that had me so intrigued about him. But when we collided, I was the one who fell down. He very kindly helped me up and got me brushed off. I was so in awe of him, I couldn't think of a thing to say.

"By Christ, you're a big kid!" he said, like he'd just noticed I only had about four chin whiskers. And that I was a good head taller than he was. "Figures you'd trip over your own feet. How old are you, anyway?"

"S-s-sixteen, just turned," I finally got out.

"Probably your shoe size, too," he muttered before he said, "Your pa know you're walkin' the streets of Tombstone at three in the a. of m. on a Saturday night? All you're liable to run into is miscreants and trash." He had a drawl, like he had come from the South. I later learned that he had.

"My daddy is murdered, Mr. Holliday, sir." I didn't go into particulars.

He kind of scrunched up his face and said, "You know me, boy? Have we been properly introduced?"

Just then, a drunk stumbled into him from the back and knocked him forward a couple of feet. I sidestepped the both of them, but Doc whipped out his pistol and banged the drunk over the head so fast I didn't realize it had happened until it was over with and the drunk lay at our feet.

"Murdered, you say? That's a tough blow for a lad of just-turned-sixteen to take. Well, close your mouth, boy, and come on in," he said, pushing open the nearest door, which belonged to the Golden Ace saloon.

"I reckon everybody in the Territory knows you, Doc," I said, with my mouth feeling like cotton.

He guided me toward a table. "Let's have a drink. Or a soda pop, at least."

Well, he ordered. He had several whiskeys and I had a sarsaparilla—I was relieved, because I had never had hard liquor in my life—and he asked me questions and I told him about what I've told you so far. I even told him that I admired him a whole lot and that I wanted to be like him.

"A worthy goal," he said after a long bit of chin rubbing. "Except I don't recommend you follow in my footsteps so far as to contract consumption. Most aggravatin', coughing up blood all the time. And don't go staring at me like that. Those eyes of yours are about to freeze me to death."

Since Ruby Tulayne was fond of telling me about the same thing, I did as he asked. In fact, I glanced down just in time to hear him say, "Well, Wyatt, you old son of a dog! Have a seat and make the acquaintance of my new friend, young Paddy Doyle!"

*   *   *

Now, Wyatt turned out to be the famous Wyatt Earp of the celebrated Earp brothers, and part of the legal contingent in town. Wyatt also part-owned the Oriental Saloon and dealt faro there. I had already met his brother, Virgil, the town's law, right after my daddy got shot. And after Doc made me repeat my story to him, and he asked me questions and such, I got to admiring him quite a bit, too. Even more than Doc, I guess, though I still held them both in high esteem.

Anyhow, it was during this conversation that I decided I didn't want to be a gambler and a shootist. First of all, I didn't know the first thing about either profession. Memorizing all those odds, like I guess you had to do if you wanted to make any good as a gambler, seemed too hard and too taxing on a brain as poor and simple as mine. I suppose that learning to shoot would have been some easier, but I didn't own a gun, and the Earps had made it a law that you couldn't carry one in town. I asked Wyatt about it.

"Well," he said, "it seems to me that if a man wanted to learn how to use a gun—and he should, just as a matter of principle—but then he left it out on the edge of town—say, by the cribs—when he came into town proper, that wouldn't offend the law any." It was like he knew my whole life history. His brother, the sheriff, had told him, I guess.

I didn't exactly know if Wyatt was a sheriff or a deputy or a marshal or if it just ran in the family, so I said, "Thank you, Mr. Earp. I appreciate the advice."

I pushed back my chair. It was about time for Ruby to let me in for the night, and I was pretty tired. "Good night, Doc, and thanks for the sody pop. It was real nice meetin' you. I hope we get to talk again."

Of course, Doc was pretty drunk by then, so I had to be satisfied with a grunt and a nod by way of an answer. I tipped my hat and made my way back to Ruby Tulayne's.

I haven't told you very much about Ruby Tulayne, save that she was a soiled dove who gave me shelter and taught me to read and write. And that she was older than me. She was twenty-eight going on twenty-nine, and before she came west, she had gone through school all the way through the eighth grade. In those days, you could be qualified to teach if you had an eighth-grade certification, and she had come to town with hopes of making a living at the chalkboard.

But the town was mostly miners—and mostly men, for that matter—and the only work she could find was on her back. Anyhow, that's how she told it.

In the beginning, her and me never had what you would call sexual congress. She said I was just a kid, and to tell you the truth, I was fair scared to death of her. She was pretty, though. She had a whole lot of real curly reddish blond hair, what I think they call strawberry blond, and it was all wild around her face when she took it down, like fairy curls. Her lashes were long and sorrel-colored. I remember watching them fluttering on her cheeks as she slept.

She was so good at heart that she didn't charge me so much as a three-cent nickel for teaching me my letters. She said it was good practice for her, and I was a good detriment to men stopping by unannounced after or before hours.

Also, she allowed as how I was a quick study, and I practiced my reading and writing a lot. There were books you could buy and read about all kinds of thrilling things, like ones about Doc Holliday or Buffalo Bill Cody or Panhandle Slim or Boss Brennan and the Navajo Whoop-Up.

I will always be grateful to Miss Ruby Tulayne for so kindly bringing me into that world of letters and words, and I believe she will always be grateful to me (or so she said) for being the only male human, outside her father, who had never tried to get into her knickers without an invitation first.

At the time, I thought it was a funny thing to be grateful for, but I guess you live and learn.

She had misty green eyes, just on the edge of

hazel, and what they used to call a "bee-stung" mouth, all tiny and pretty and pouty. Ruby was what they called a "looker," and I never understood why she worked the tent city when she could have made a lot more cash money in the saloons. Maybe she wanted to keep all the money for herself. I know she kept a coffee can stashed underneath her cot, and she used to stuff all her money inside it.

I wasn't supposed to know about it, but I did. I woke once in the dark, hard night to see her standing over her bed in the feeble light of the moon, putting money in that can, then hiding it again. I pretended to be asleep.

To my way of thinking, what people want to do with their money is their own business, and if she trusted Mr. Arbuckle's can with her cash, that was good enough for me.

Well, it was that night I talked with Doc and Wyatt that sort of turned my life around. All of a sudden I didn't want to be like Doc so much as Wyatt. Not a marshal or a sheriff, exactly, but fast with a gun, and respected not only because of that but because I was on the right side of things, I guess. When you sat down and listened to Wyatt for a while, you just knew he was on the right side of things.

I suppose it said quite a bit for Doc that him and Wyatt were friends like they were. That impressed me, too, but not that Wyatt was Doc's friend. It was that Doc was Wyatt's.

Anyway, by the next morning I had set the whole course of my life. That's how I thought of it, anyway. I'd be a real fast hand with a gun, and I'd be in the right. I know that sounds kind of simple, but it was a whole lot more appealing than taking orders from Old Man Thorogood for the rest of my days.

The first thing I had to do was buy a gun. Now, I had about seventeen dollars saved up, so I took myself to the gunsmith's shop and did some looking around. There were sure a lot of kinds: the old ball and powder pistols, and single- or double-barreled shotguns, rifles, and six-shooters, and center-firing pins and rimfire guns . . . When that poor clerk was done explaining it all to me, we both had to sit down for a while. He had a couple drags on his flask, too.

Of course, about half of what he said went whizzing over my head, but I finally got across that I wanted a kind of gun reputed to be easy to draw, and accurate, and not too expensive.

He picked me out a used ebony-butted Colt of the Peacemaker model, and then spent about an hour trying to find just the right belt and holster for me. He said that holster part was more important to the draw than the gun, and the one he finally deemed right for me turned out to be a simple belt with a plain holster that had been cut down lower than it had started out. There was a little strap on it meant to go around the hammer and help hold the gun in place.

The man said to always keep that strap on the gun unless I was going to shoot something, and he also advised me to load it with only five bullets, even though there was room for six. Said I was liable to shoot my own knee off otherwise.

After he showed me how to load it, and then sold me a couple boxes of cartridges, he had all my savings and I had the gun, the belt, and enough ammunition to shoot up a whole field of cactus.

I thought it was a pretty fair trade.

2

Now, I have said that my daddy only taught me my numbers and that he couldn't write for spit. But I'm here to tell you that he wasn't anybody's fool. For one thing, he taught me to speak the Irish, which after all was his native tongue. He had also picked up a little Welsh from working the mines for so long, shoulder to shoulder with all those Welsh miners, and this he taught me, too. Those, plus a smidge of Mexican he gave me, along with my English. I think that was pretty dang good for a man with no formal schooling.

I'm telling you about my daddy now, because he was the most important thing in the world to me, and you need to understand that when he was took so callous and cruel, I had nothing to fill that empty space with, except for Ruby Tulayne's lessons and thoughts of growing up to be like Daddy and Wyatt and Doc, all rolled into one.

I have told you I had his height—maybe a couple inches more by the time I was fully grown—and his eyes, but I also had his hair. It was coal black, and grew in loose ringlets on our heads. Well, mine was a little more lank, I guess. He always said that I got my golden skin from my mama—his was closer to a cool pink, really fair—and my way of humming when I was thinking, too.

And I had a lot of thinking to do.

But I'm getting ahead of myself. I have a sort of tendency to do that, sometimes. I was talking about Tombstone, and learning to use a gun.

Every afternoon, after me and Ruby Tulayne got up and she made some coffee and wrote out my assignment for the day, I'd grab up the flour sack I kept my gun belt and schoolwork in and carry it out of town, to a place where there was a big field of prickly pear cactus.

I liked to shoot at those. One, because you just couldn't kill the dang things. If you shot a pad, or part of one, clear off the plant, sooner or later it would just sprout where it landed. I daresay that somewhere down by Tombstone, there's still a whole couple acres of prickly pear that I planted personally.

The second reason was that they were easy to

hit. Those pads can be a foot long, and are real broad and flat. After a while, I got so I could hit one dead center, and then I got to where I could just slice 'em off at the place where the newer pad had grown out of the top of the older one. I thought I was really something, let me tell you.

But the other thing about cactus is that it don't move, and it don't shoot back. This is both a good thing and a bad thing.

Anyhow, having spent all my savings and wishing to be no burden on Ruby Tulayne, I found part-time work sweeping out the Oriental Saloon, in the employ of none other than Wyatt Earp himself. Wyatt was good to work for. He paid me fair and also never yelled at me, except for the one time when I emptied the spittoon out the front door and right onto his boots.

Even then, he didn't shout very long and he ended up not firing me, but only said that I should look before I flung.

He'd also ask me from time to time how my target practice was coming along.

I'd always answer, "Fair to middlin', sir."

And he'd always say that one day he'd ride out and watch me.

He never did, though. I suppose things can be hectic for a man when his brother's the marshal and he's always fightin' the town politics plus runnin' a whole saloon *and* being tied up in a fast-moving real estate market. The Earps were out to take over the whole town, and if you asked me, they couldn't do it fast enough.

Some folks might have disagreed with me on that, but what with the alternative being dandified lawmen like Johnny Behan or roughnecks and cattle thieves like the Clantons and the McLaurys and Johnny Ringo, I think that most were on my side of the question.

I stayed at Miss Ruby Tulayne's crib for a little more than six months—well, maybe seven—before I got to thinking I was overstaying my welcome and moved to the Russ House, which was run by one Miss Nellie Cashman. I liked Miss Nellie. She was a real kind person, especially to the miners who were, more often than not, down on their luck. She was swell to me, and didn't even mind that I was taking my lessons with Ruby Tulayne.

Miss Nellie—who was so short that she didn't much come up past my belt—said that it didn't matter where you got your learning, so long as you had the guts to get it.

Of course, by that time I was getting another kind of learning from Ruby, but I didn't mention it. Ruby didn't charge me for that, either, God bless her.

But we were taking up too much of her "bread and butter" time, and having no wish to drive her into poverty, I went to stay at the Russ House. I missed her company, but at least it was a shorter walk to work at the Oriental by about a mile, and I didn't have to walk through the tent city every day.

I don't think I told you about the tent city, did I? It went around the town proper kind of like a doughnut goes around a hole. It was thick and confusing, and milling with all sorts of unseemly types, such as opium smokers, con men, prostitutes without such good hearts as Ruby's—men and women who'd kill you for a two-cent nickel and be glad of a good day's wages.

The center of town was real nice, though. There, it wasn't tents and sheds, but was so fresh and brand-new that you could practically smell the paint drying. There were mostly wood buildings, some of them real fancy, and the streets were wide, not narrow, twisty alleys like in the tent city.

The main road, which was called Allen, was especially interesting, because one side of it was all nice places—good restaurants and dressmakers and haberdashers and gunsmiths and the like, all with tidy fronts and big glass windows. The opposite side was, almost to a building, whorehouses or saloons or both. Painted women—ugly and beautiful, old and young— used to hang out the windows all hours of the day and night, beckoning to passersby to the discordant music of ill-tuned pianos and fiddles and mouth harps.

Although it later dried up into the next thing to a ghost town, I recall somebody saying that at that time it was about as big, population-wise, as San Francisco. I don't know about that, but it was sure and enough the wildest, wide-openest, rip-roaringest mining town I had ever lived in. And I felt like I had lived in most of them.

The Earps were doing their best to clean it up, though. They had "dead lines" set up at all roads that led in or out of the doughnut hole, and you weren't supposed to carry a firearm past those points. Most ignored the rule, but at least they made a point of keeping their guns concealed. Me, I kept mine in town, but under my mattress at Miss Nellie's boardinghouse.

Anyway, one afternoon while I was walking up to the Oriental to go to work, I noticed a big mob of people stopped stock-still and all staring over toward the alley between Fly's Photography and the OK Corral.

By the time I shouldered my way to the front of the crowd, I had sure enough missed the show, and what a show it must have been! There stood Wyatt, helping his brother Virgil to his feet with the assistance of Morgan Earp. Doc Holliday stood over to the side a bit, his still-smoking shotgun dangling from his hand. There were a few dead men lying there, too, in that narrow lot.

Suddenly somebody grabbed my arm and spun me around.

"The Earps started it, didn't they, kid? You seen it plain as day!" he hollered in my ear before he yelled, "He seen it, too, just ask him!" at a lady behind me in the crowd.

I shook off Sheriff Behan like he was a pesky terrier. "I didn't see anything, sir," I said, and that was the truth of it. "If you want a lot of witnesses, you'd best do something about slowing down the shoot-outs in this town."

The woman, who had probably gone through much the same thing with Behan, said, "That's right, Sheriff! Don't know why you're down here, anyway."

A man in the crowd said, "That's right, Johnny. Go on and have another beer."

Behan looked around for the speaker, but didn't have any luck. The crowd was dispersing by then.

I don't think the whole battle took more than maybe thirty seconds. A minute, tops. Behan's questions took up more time than the shooting had.

Behan stepped forward, out into the street, and had words with Wyatt, Virgil being propped between Wyatt and Morgan. I couldn't hear what was said, but Wyatt must have won the verbal battle because Behan backed off and let them pass, along with Doc. I remember that Doc winked at me as he went by.

And me? I went on up to the Oriental and started my day's work. But I was thinking. Thinking about Tombstone, and why I had stayed on after Daddy got shot. It didn't seem to me to be the safest place around, when even the marshal could get winged over who knew what.

I didn't find out until later that night who the dead men were. The Clanton and McLaury outfits had surely suffered that day, and all because they had to come into town, bold as brass, wearing their guns like dares on their hips.

It wasn't more than a week before I left town and headed north, carrying everything I owned in my saddlebags and riding a new horse named Consternation. Actually, he wasn't all that new, being fifteen and a year younger than me, and his saddle and bridle cost more than he did. But he was a good-natured beast, easygoing, with a quiet way about him.

On my way out of town, I rode past Wyatt, talking to a little knot of men, and he held up his hand for me to stop. I did.

"That Lop Ear Tommy Cleveland's sorrel gelding you're ridin'?" he asked, one of his brows arched.

"I don't know any Mr. Cleveland," I replied.

"I bought Consternation from a horse trader down at the Fair Deal livery."

"Leave it to Lop Ear to trade off a good horse," Wyatt said, and gave his head a shake. "He's a fool for a mule, old Lop Ear is. Just got a new one. Don't suppose he could afford to feed 'em both."

Now, the conversation had drifted too far for me to ever be able to catch it again, so I just tipped my hat and said, "I'd best be goin'. Nice knowin' you, Wyatt."

"Good luck to you, boy," he said, and waved me good-bye.

Now, I hadn't taken my leave of Tombstone lightly, nor leaving Ruby Tulayne nor my job or my new friends at Miss Nellie's. I had "searched my soul" like the poets say, but I ended up saying a teary and heartfelt good-bye to Ruby, and a more manly fare-thee-well to the others.

And to be honest, I didn't want to stay around for the trial. Behan was pushing the point, and it looked like Doc and the Earps would stand trial for shooting those skunk-butt outlaws. I figured I couldn't be of any help to them, but a crafty lawyer might trick me into saying something harmful. Daddy hadn't much love for lawyers, and neither did I.

I had thought a lot about where to travel. I sure didn't want to be a miner, but that only told me where I shouldn't be, not where I should. Daddy, whose killer had never been found, had told me more times than I could think of that my ma died giving me life. He hadn't even told me her name.

But I figured I wasn't so old that there might not be somebody still living 'round where we had in the San Francisco Peaks, somebody who might know who she'd been or what she'd been called by. Especially if she'd been a soiled dove, like Daddy had said.

Men don't forget a good prostitute. (He always said that, too.)

Anyhow, it was something to do.

3

Contrary to what most folks—the ones who aren't from Arizona, anyway—think, the San Francisco Peaks are here, up north in Arizona and in no way farther west, near the town of San Francisco. At least, I don't think so. I was headed toward the old mining town of Greased Weasel in the San Francisco Range, if it was still there. The town, that was.

You couldn't count on mining towns staying around for long back in those years.

These, either, come to think of it.

But after two weeks and two days of rambling northward and finding and losing mountain trails and asking questions whenever I got the chance, I found it, just a few up-and-down miles north of Flagstaff. Or what was left of it, anyhow.

There were lots of falling-down shacks turned into kindling, or deadfalls inhabited only by wood rats, lizards, or snakes. But a little farther down the trail, I found a couple of old cabins that looked like they might still have folks living in them.

I stepped down off Consternation—who had turned out to be a real nice mount—and called, "Hello, the houses!" but nobody came out. I led my horse forward and knocked on the front door of the first one.

"Hello?" I asked, then hollered.

There was no answer.

I put a hand on the latch, then paused. This place looked lived in, and if Daddy could have seen me, ready to walk straight into a stranger's house, he would have skinned me alive.

So I walked on a few paces to the littler shack huddled under the next tree and repeated the whole process.

Nobody was home there, either.

"Consternation," I said as I mounted back up, "I can't believe that the whole population has run off all of a sudden. Let's keep tryin'."

He didn't say no, so we kept following the trail, which took a hard right after about twenty yards and then opened up into something nearer to what I'd call a town. Not a real town, mind you, but it was a mite closer than the two vacant lean-tos back down the trail. Also there was a bleached-out, busted sign that said WEL-COME TO GREASED WEASEL.

This time I didn't dismount before I called out

to the houses. There were seven of them, all small, with three on the uphill side of the road and four on the downhill. Even though the trail had been widened into something closer to a road and the trees had been cut back to accommodate it, the ponderosa pines still towered overhead, throwing most of the place into deep shadows.

In fact, I heard the old man before I saw him. "Up here!" he hollered again, waving his arms so I'd see him. He was wire-thin, looked to be older than the mountain he was standing on, and was dressed in the same color of clothing as the paint on the house he'd just stepped out of—weather-beaten gray. "What you want from an old man?"

I rode toward him, calling, "Sorry to bother you, sir," while my eyes flicked from one house to the next. I could swear the curtains moved in one of their windows. "I was born in these parts. My daddy—Paddy Doyle was his name—he used to work at the mine."

He stepped down off his front stoop and came out to meet me. I got down off Consternation again, and the little man just stood there and stared up at me for a spell.

"Well, I'll be damned," he finally said. "You're sure his spittin' image."

I felt a great big grin spreading over my face. Here was the first person I'd found who had known my daddy good enough to remember what he looked like!

"You got yourself a name, young feller?" he asked.

"Patrick Doyle, same's my daddy," I replied.

Just then, another cabin's front door burst open, and as I turned toward it, a woman's voice called out, "Who's that out there with you, Edgar?" She was even shorter than him, although she was dressed a mite prettier.

"Hold on to your bustle, Elmira!" he hollered down her way, then said, "I'm Edgar Conklin. Knew your daddy fairly well. And that old harridan what just hollered at you is Elmira Smudge Higgins. Mind you remember all three of them names. She gets mad and holds on to it, Elmira does. You don't have to live here, but I do."

The light, already thin, was failing pretty good by that time, and since he showed no signs of asking me inside, I went ahead and lit into my subject. "Mr. Conklin, I'm hopin' you can answer a question or two for me. I rode a long ways to find this place."

He hiked a brow. "This place? Don't you even know the name'a the town you're in?"

I wouldn't have really called it a town, but I said, "Greased Weasel. Just kind of how to get here."

"Well, the name'a the place is Mourning Dove.

Mourning Dove, Arizona Territory. Used to be called Greased Weasel, but the name got changed 'bout fifteen, sixteen years back. On account of your daddy. On account of you."

I just stood there with my mouth hanging open, eyes blinking.

By then, the old woman had walked up right behind me and said, "You turn 'round again, boy."

Slowly, I craned myself about. She looked like a nasty little piece of business, like she was never one tiny bit less mad than a wet frog on a hot stove lid.

"What'd he do this time?" she snarled. "Send you back here to break more hearts, ruin more lives?"

"N-no, ma'am," I stuttered. I had forgot her name entirely. I tied Consternation to a post near Conklin's doorway, then added, "And my daddy didn't send me nowhere. He's dead."

"It ain't *ma'am*!" she hollered, still all het up. "It's either Miss Elmira or Mrs. Smudge Higgins, and I'm glad your daddy's dead. Now, come on over to my house, you two. You're both 'bout as skin and bones as a couple'a wormy coyotes."

Now, while the name "wormy coyote" kind of fit Edgar Conklin, it in no way described me, and it got me a little angry. I told Mr. Conklin as much as he pushed me after Mrs. Elmira

Smudge Higgins. Well, I told him I didn't appreciate her talking about me, anyway!

"Shut up," he hissed, and poked me in the back again. "I seen her killin' a hen this forenoon. Mayhap she's got a stew on!"

She had a "stew on" all right, but it didn't have anything to do with chickens, if you asked me. Anyhow, that's what I was thinking as Mr. Conklin pushed me up the porch steps behind Mrs. Elmira Smudge Higgins.

She had a pretty nice house, all filled with the good smell of chicken stew. I reckon she was pretty comfortable there. I wondered if anybody else lived in town, or if they were keeping me all to themselves. Maybe to lynch later on, by way of dessert.

Anyway, nobody spoke so much as a word while we ate. It was real fine—seasoned up all homey with carrots and peas and onions—and she had some crackerjack biscuits to go with it, all light and flaky. Also a tub of honey the size of a nail keg. I figured that Mr. Conklin must not get asked to dinner very often, because he was so skinny. He ate like there was never going to be a tomorrow.

When I was done eating, I rubbed my stomach and said, "Best I've had, Mrs. Smudge Higgins," to appear sociable, and also because it was the truth.

She looked over at me for the first time since

we'd sat down and said, "You're exactly like your daddy. Full'a compliments and fancified talk he was, too."

Mr. Conklin leaned toward me and softly added, "Elmira's daughter was once affianced to ol' Paddy. He done left town without a word."

"Left and took you with him," Mrs. Smudge Higgins huffed before she took a sip of her coffee. "With nary a word to poor Clementine. Nary one word!" She glowered at Mr. Conklin like he was the one who done it.

And then she turned that gaze on me. "Left in the middle of the night. Even left that little Indian whore all alone up there."

"She weren't all Indian, Elmira, and don't be gettin' cruel with this boy. Ain't his fault. He were just a babe."

Well, they had lost me, and I told them so. Was Mrs. Smudge Higgins—my grandma? I sure hoped not. Who was this Indian whore? And why on earth would my daddy scoot off in the middle of the night?

"There's somebody I think you oughter meet, Paddy Junior," said Mr. Conklin.

I couldn't get a read on him. His face was that still. I would have bet he was good at poker.

I asked, "Who would that be, sir?"

Elmira Smudge Higgins wouldn't be so good at cards, though. She shot him a look across the table that would have knocked any other man to the floor. "Don't you dare, Edgar Conklin! One of them's enough for anybody to have to take."

"What?" I yelped. "What do you mean by that?"

"Your d-daddy was—" stammered Mr. Conklin.

"—a big, evil, prevaricatin' liar alongside bein' a baby stealer." Mrs. Smudge Higgins broke in. She crossed her arms and set her jaw, like that was all there was going to be, period.

I just sat there for a couple seconds, trying to think what to say, and then it came to me, just like that. "Mrs. Smudge Higgins, I ain't my daddy. He's dead and buried, for one thing, God rest his soul. I don't think it's nice of you to go round defamin' the dead, especially to his own kin's face."

Well, I was a little rougher on her than I meant to be, and when I stopped I just sat there, quiet, and so did she, though she didn't look at me. Mr. Conklin had turned all white and appeared about to bolt, though.

"Now, who's this person I should meet, Mr. Conklin?" I asked.

He answered real small, so that I couldn't really hear him. I said, "Say again?"

"Your mama, for to start with," he replied. It was like he had a frog in his throat the size of a groundhog.

"My . . . my mama?"

"Don't know what your daddy told you, Junior," broke in Elmira, kind of nasty, "but your ma's alive and well, and living out back of the old Good Times whorehouse with your brother. If the crazy sonofabuck ain't skipped town yet."

I blinked. "There was two of me?" I squeaked in a way I hadn't since I was twelve and my voice changed. How was this possible?

Mr. Conklin pushed back his chair. "Still are," he said, trying to smile and failing dismally. "Right good hen, Elmira. I'm obliged to be asked to dinner."

She didn't answer, just hugged her skinny chest harder.

I remembered my manners. "Yes'm. Thank you most kindly."

She muttered something under her breath, but I didn't get a chance to ask her to repeat herself, for Edgar Conklin fair dragged me from the cabin.

"You just don't know what's good for you, Junior," he hissed once we'd reached the safety of the yard. It was so dark out there that I couldn't have seen a barn owl if it was sitting on my nose.

Mr. Conklin lit a match, which made me jump. "Get your horse. We're goin' to town."

Town? I thought this was it, or at least what

was left of it, but I located Consternation while Mr. Conklin found his old lantern, and after lighting it, he began to lead me down the road.

Mourning Dove wasn't more than a half mile 'round the bend, but I was sure glad Mr. Conklin had brought along his lantern. Due to there being no moon, coupled with the thickness of the bough and limb overhang, the road was about as dark as the inside of a black hog.

"A brother?" I asked in a whisper, even though we were well away from Mrs. Smudge Higgins. I was still fair stunned at the news.

"Older'n you by about a year, I reckon," Conklin muttered. He took a little hop to the left. "Watch where you step. That there's a dead opossum."

I moved to the left, too, and led Consternation around the moldering corpse, which wriggled with maggots.

I must have made some guttural sound, because over his shoulder he said, "Don't puke on them new boots'a your'n."

They weren't hardly new, having been passed to me by my daddy, but I didn't say anything. The "town" was beginning to come into view.

It wasn't much to talk about, and probably never had been, even back when the mine was going full tilt. As it stood, I made out the shapes of five, maybe six, wide-spaced houses. Not much farther on, we found what had been stores, I guess. Somebody was burning leaves, and although I couldn't see the fire, the smoke smelled nice. I remarked on it.

"That's probably that goddamn Harley Soames again," Conklin said in a disapproving tone. "Always wantin' to 'neaten up' his place, he is. Always burnin' or paintin' or shorin' up stuff."

It sounded like a good idea to me, but I was smart enough to keep my mouth shut. It looked to be the saloon coming up next, in the shadows over to the right side.

Mr. Conklin suddenly cut in front of me and called out, "Faye! Faye Reynaud!"

There was a creak as somebody opened a door back behind the saloon, and then the shape of a cloaked woman appeared. Tall and willowy and graceful as she moved toward us, she reminded me of something out of a book. I imagined Guinevere from King Arthur, which I'd just started to read.

As me and Mr. Conklin moved toward her, the shadow over her face got a lot deeper and darker, then vanished. She was an Indian—I didn't know what kind—and she was just plain beautiful.

"Junior," announced Mr. Conklin, breaking whatever spell I was momentarily under, "this here's your mama. Faye, meet the boy that Ol' Paddy made off with."

I didn't know what to say. I just stood there.

But Faye knew what to do. She stepped right forward and threw her arms around me and said, "My boy, my baby boy," over and over again.

I still couldn't say anything, but I hugged her back. That seemed to make her happy enough for the time being. And then I saw another figure approach from where she'd come.

He was tall and slim, and for a minute, when he walked into the feeble light of Conklin's lantern, I would have sworn it was a mirror. He looked that much like me. Except he had light brown eyes, not blue.

"Mother," he said. Not like a question, like a statement of fact.

The woman let go of me and latched on to him. She stroked his face and said, "Patrick, my Patrick. This is your brother, who was taken from us when he was still wet and bloody from his passage into this world."

4

To tell you the honest truth, I was plumb stuck for something to say. First off, there was my brother, standing not five feet from me. Second of all, there was my ma, an Indian, with her arms around him and calling him my name!

It was like that mountain opened up right under my feet and swallowed me down into some dark pit. I kind of wished it would, too.

Somehow, although I wasn't aware of my feet moving, or even me moving at all, we all walked around the back of the saloon and into her little house and sat down in the parlor.

There was a fire going in the hearth, so I couldn't see my breath anymore, and the cold began to ease out of my joints and my fingers. It got awful cold come night up in those mountains. After a long while of us just sitting there and looking at each other, I took off my coat and said, "I never in my wildest dreams thought that I had a real brother, but there you are."

Patrick didn't answer. He only scowled at me. I sure hoped I didn't look like that when I was annoyed with somebody, but I suppose I did. Except for the eyes, it was like looking in a dang looking glass—maybe one that was a little too wavy, but still a looking glass.

My ma said, "We welcome you to your home, my son," and clasped my hands in hers. They were long and slender, like she was, but rough from hard work. I could see in her what she had been all those years ago, though, and why my daddy had been attracted.

I muttered, "Thank you, ma'am."

And she smiled and said, "You may call me Mother. I am, you know, even though you never slept upon my breast."

I think I must've flushed, 'cause my face went all hot. "Yes, Ma," I whispered, and then I'll be danged if my eyes didn't start to pool up. The next thing I knew, I was hanging on to her for dear life and bawling like a baby.

When at last I looked up, Patrick had disappeared—he was likely embarrassed at having such a crybaby for a brother. I can't say I blamed him. Anyhow, I would have been. Mr. Conklin was gone, too, so there was just me and Ma.

You know, I'm used to saying that now—

"Ma," I mean—but right then it had a sort of eerie newness to it.

She sat back and studied my face. "How is your father?"

Without thinking, I said, "Dead, ma'am. He got shot. That's why I come to find you."

Her face went all quiet-like—no sadness or mourning or emotion whatsoever—just quiet, like a sheltered pond on a windless day. I have seen her be a lot of things since, but that's how I'll always remember her, the way she looked just then.

I took her hand. "I'm awful sorry to be so straight out with it. I didn't think, I guess."

"You are but a boy, *cher*," she said. I guess my face must have scrunched up some, on account of not understanding that last word she used, but she smiled and patted my hand, and added, "*Cher*, it is just a term of endearment. I may not look it, but my father was French."

"You could'a fooled me. I thought you was all Injun."

"Crow, on my mother's side. Father was a trapper, from up Canada way. He found my mother in the mountains of California, raped and left for dead. Father was a good man. He saved her, fell in love with her, and married her, although she was never right in the head after that."

She told it matter-of-factly, but I still ducked

my head and said, "I'm right sorry, ma'am. I mean, Ma. Right sorry to hear that about your mother."

"*Que sera, sera*," she said, then asked, "Have you eaten?"

When I nodded yes, she seemed to realize we were in an empty room and muttered, "Now, where has that Patrick gone off to? Probably out with his colt, if I know him. You know, he takes after my mother. Always hearing voices. Do you?"

"N-no, ma'am," I said and scraped my chair back. "I should go out there, shouldn't I?"

"I believe you should."

When I went out, it didn't take much looking to find him, forking straw in the little barn they had. I walked in and stood there for a minute, waiting on him to acknowledge me, but he just kept forking straw, and when the stall was knee-high in it, turned to filling the hay manger.

So I said, "Ma's right pretty, isn't she?"

"Don't you call her your ma," he growled without so much as looking at me.

"Don't know what else to call her. She's my mama, sure's shootin'."

There was a long silence, cut only by his horse's molars on hay, before he asked, "So, what do you want?"

"Want?" I took a scratch at the back of my

head. "Don't reckon I want anything. 'Cept to meet her. And you, too, of course. Even if I didn't know there was a you."

"Well, you done both, so you can leave anytime, now," he said, picking up a body brush. He began to work on the horse's flank. He raised quite a bit of dust, too.

"Patrick, that's no way to talk to your brother." We both twisted round to see Ma standing in the doorway, a lantern in her hand. "The very least we owe him is a good dinner and a place to sleep for the night."

"I already et, Ma. Mrs. Elmira Smudge Higgins gave both me and Mr. Conklin some good chicken stew and biscuits and such."

She lifted her brows. "Are you still hungry? Elmira can be niggardly with her vittles."

"No, Ma, I got plenty. I thank you for asking, though." I doffed my hat, I think.

"Well, you can share Patrick's room for the night, and tomorrow morning I'll fix a big breakfast. It'll give us more time to talk, *cher*. Patrick, are you all right?" When he nodded, she smiled, then turned on her heel and vanished into the night.

I guess I dug my toe in the dirt some before I said, "I'm sorry, Patrick. About havin' to share your room, I mean. I can sleep out here just fine." I pointed to the heap of straw he'd been forking from earlier.

Either he didn't hear me or didn't care to answer, because he said, "What am I supposed to call you?"

I almost said "Patrick" until I realized that he might think I was swiping his identity as well as his mama, so I said, "Paddy's fine. Or Junior. Or J.R."

"All right, Junior. Don't mind you sleepin' in my room, so long as you take the floor."

"Fine with me," I said, quicker than I ought. Except for Miss Nellie Cashman's boarding-house, I had slept my whole life on floors. I figured that at least this one would be dry and not made of gravel or dirt.

"You said you rode on up from Tombstone," he went on, more to his gelding than to me.

"Yup."

He nodded like he knew the route. Maybe he did, for all I knew.

"That Elmira Smudge Higgins," I said. "Mr. Conklin said she had a daughter that was engaged to our pa. Anything come of it?"

For the first time, Patrick smiled a little. "Like another brother, you mean?"

I shrugged. "I dunno. I was just wonderin'."

"She wed up with a liquor salesman," he said, brushing away. "Took off in the middle of the night without a word to her ma. Reckon that's why ol' Elmira's still mad."

"Oh." There wasn't much else to say, except

for asking if I could bring Consternation into the barn and give him a feed.

"Don't see why not," Patrick said. "Might's well be stuck with your nag, too."

Well, later on, after Consternation was put in the smaller side stall and hayed and grained and brushed down, me and Patrick repaired to the house. I must have sat up half the night talking to Ma, and she was a fine lady, indeed.

Her daddy had been a French trapper and her ma a Crow squaw, and she had all kinds of stories from her growing up to tell me. She asked about my dad, too, and I told her all I knew. Which I came to realize wasn't very much, not compared to what she had to tell about her childhood and all the mountain men getting together at Rendezvous and how she filled the quiet months in between. Her pa, she said, had been taken by a crazed grizzly bear while she hid in the woodbox, like she'd been told. She was seven then.

She told about burying what was left of her pa, and she and her ma headed south. Come a few years later (which she left most of out), her ma was dead, she had taken to whoring, and she found herself in this little town that would one day be named for her. Or at least for her sorrow.

I told her I sure wished my daddy had stayed

with her. I meant it, too. And she cried a little. I did too, I guess.

We were both real tired by then, so she sent me off to bed and pointed out Patrick's room. "When Patrick was eleven," she said, "I sent him down to Flagstaff, to that boys' boarding school they have. That's when his troubles started. They sent him packing in less than a month, after he tried to set the dormitory on fire. Ain't been exactly right since, but you won't hold it against him, will you, *cher*?"

I didn't rightly figure what she was talking about, but I shook my head and said, "No, ma'am." She kissed my forehead.

I took the stub of a candle with me, so as not to trip over the furnishings with my big old feet, and found that Patrick had laid me out some quilts and blankets with which to make a pallet on the floor. I did.

I thought I had done real good not to wake him, and was still congratulating myself when I snuggled into my makeshift bed and blew out the candle. And I'll be danged if just as I was nodding off, he didn't say, "You're not asleep, are you?"

I allowed as how I wasn't, and then he started in. By God, he could talk! I guess it was easier for him when he didn't have to look at me, either, because for me, talking to him was like talking into a looking glass.

He'd been listening to Ma and me talk, he said, and he was all excited. See, he knew some of where Daddy'd been before he came to the San Francisco Peaks, but not as much as Ma had told me of it, or what parts I'd added on to fill in the gaps.

He said, "If Daddy dropped a litter here and run off, who's to say he didn't do it before? What you say you and me backtrack him and have a look-see?"

I thought it over real careful for a whole half second before I said, "Yes!" I was wanting to see some countryside anyhow, and how better to see it than with my brother?

"We'll leave in the morning, then," he said.

"Night, Patrick," I replied, and pulled the covers over my head.

"Night, Junior," I thought he said.

I let it go at that.

5

The way it turned out, we ate breakfast with Ma and the three of us talked and talked, and by the time Patrick told her we were leaving, she didn't throw much of a fuss at all. It surprised me, and I told Patrick as much while we saddled up.

But he told me, "Aw, she was expectin' it. They said so."

I didn't see how she could have been—or who "they" were—but I didn't ask any further.

We led the horses out front and both of us hugged Ma and kissed her good-bye. She gave us a sack of vittles but cried nary a tear, and before I knew it, we were clean shed of Mourning Dove and headed northeast, toward Colorado.

Now, it was my brother Patrick's notion to backtrack Pa's path to Mourning Dove in reverse chronological order. I wanted to do it geographically—the closest first, no matter when he'd been there. But Patrick being my elder, I gave in and let him run things.

This was something I would live to regret, but at the time it didn't cause much problem.

I had brought my books along, and had talked Patrick into letting me borrow some of his. He allowed as how this was kind of odd—me wanting to read while we were off on such a big adventure, that is—but like me letting him take charge, he put up with it.

He'd be sorry he did this, too.

About two weeks after leaving Mourning Dove—and after three primers and two Buffalo Bill books and a Bible chapter every night—we finally approached the half-dead town of Silver Rapids, Colorado. I could see where it had been a thriving community because it boasted three whorehouses, or the remnants of them, on one side of the main street alone.

Me and Patrick hadn't seen a soul as yet, but we didn't waste any time. We started in town. He took one side of the street and I took the other.

It looked as if he was having better luck than I was. He turned up a woman with three kids and an old man while I was still batting zero, and was engaged in a lengthy palaver with the old man when I raised my knuckles to the dusty door of what had been a dry-goods store.

My knuckles never touched wood, though, because all of a gol-dang sudden the door opened inward and a head poked out. A sunburnt old man with a raspy voice choked out, "I thought I told you to stop comin' 'round here, Josiah!"

I took a step back. "What? Who?"

"Don't play all innocent with me, boy! I told you before, Lannigan was here a few months back, lookin' for your no-good papa. You look enough like him that you're gonna get yourself shot iffen he spies you from a distance. You using some kind of unguent on your face?" He gave a nervous look around, then stood on tiptoes to spy over my shoulder. "Maybe he'll shoot me, too, iffen I's standin' too close. Now, git!"

The door slammed in my face. Or Josiah's face, depending on your slant on it, I guess.

I stood there for a second, shocked-like, then turned and hightailed it across the street. I met Patrick, just coming out of a tired wood building, and near knocked him down.

"Hey!" he said, all cranky.

"Who's Lannigan?" I demanded. "Who's Josiah?"

His face was as vacant as an empty lot. "Huh? And watch where you're goin', Junior!"

"Sorry. But that old man across the street said—"

The door Patrick had just come out of opened, just a pinch, and I could see part of a lady's face. "Ol' Dutch, he told you about Lannigan?" she asked in a trembling voice.

I said, "Yes'm," real quick, before Patrick had a chance to open his piehole.

She looked from him to me, then back again. "You boys sure do look like— All right. C'mon back in."

I took that to mean just Patrick, but she frowned and motioned to me to follow along, too.

She sat us down in a dusty front room, then took a chair opposite. "Leave it to Dutch, the old gossip," she muttered with a shake of her head. "You boys are sure two peas in a pod. Three in a pod, I mean. I can scarce believe it. You're lookin' for Josiah, aren'tcha."

She didn't say it at all like a question, and I just sat there. But Patrick, having talked to her before, blurted out, "Where can we find him? He's our brother. Half brother, I mean."

"I can't think he's nobody else's."

"Well, where is he?" I asked, bravado suddenly surging through my veins. I guess it was the excitement.

"Last I heard he was in the next town over. That's Possum Creek, 'bout two days north." She pointed her finger in that direction by way of emphasis. "He took off when he heard Lannigan was lookin' for his daddy."

"But who's Lannigan?" I asked. Daddy had

been shot, and right at the moment my money was on this Lannigan, whoever he was.

The old lady sighed deeply, as if she couldn't believe anybody was so dumb as I was. And then she said, "He works for the Five Points outfit. Back in New York City."

I guess both Patrick and me looked pretty blank, because she added, "The Five Points gang? Well, one of them, anyhow. They practically run New York, or used to, back around the time of the War. And before and after."

We were still pretty vacant. We looked at each other, Patrick and me, and he shrugged.

The old lady looked cross enough to smack us, but instead, she said, "Look here, boys. Your daddy come from back east, right?"

I said, "Yes'm. New York City."

"Well, I don't know what he did to cross them boys, but it must have been powerful bad for them to still be on his tail after all these years. That Lannigan, he's nothin' but trouble."

I said, "I think Lannigan already found Daddy, ma'am. He got shot and killed right in front of me, down at the Three Strikes Mine. Shot from the far-off hills."

She made the sign of the cross. "I'm sorry, then, boys. That sounds like Lannigan's style."

We set out for Possum Creek.

The nights were getting so cold I nearly froze

my feet off, and the days weren't much better. Both Patrick and I took to riding with our blankets wrapped around our shoulders and trailing down our backs, and even Patrick said, "I'm sure glad Daddy was in Nevada afore this."

"Kinda zigzagged his way around, didn't he?"

"Zigzagged like a crazy man, if you was to ask me," Patrick replied with a scowl, before he kicked his horse up a sharp slope.

And that was that.

At the end of the second day, we reached Possum Creek. It looked more thriving than Silver Rapids, but then, that didn't take much. Once again we started up opposite sides of the street, although a good bit more eagerly than before. When you find out you have a brother named Josiah—I mean, when he's real and has a name and everything—it makes you all that much more eager to turn him up in a hurry.

Anyway, it did me.

Patrick was the one who found him, though. He hollered at me from up the way, "Hey, Junior!" and when I looked up, he was standing there with his hand on the collar of a fellow that looked like a colored version of himself. Or of me. Actually, more like an octoroon version, what folks used to call "high yaller."

I fully admit that for the first few seconds, I was shocked, then ashamed, and then resigned.

And as I ran across the road to get a closer look and tell him howdy, I couldn't help but laugh out loud at myself. There I was, getting het up about Daddy sleeping with a colored woman when Patrick and me had a genuine half-Indian mama.

"Josiah!" I shouted when I was halfway there. "Patrick, you found him!"

"And more's the pity," Patrick muttered as I stepped up on the walk. "He don't want to be found."

Josiah twisted away from Patrick's restraining hand. His eyes focused on Patrick and he snarled, "I said leave go!"

Then he looked at me. He was tall like me and Patrick, but heavier built even than Daddy. Not fat, but real muscular. He looked like he tossed bulls around for fun. He was also broader in the face and fuller-lipped, and had eyes the color of coffee with cream. But Josiah sure looked enough like Patrick and me that I could forgive that old man back in Silver Rapids for mistaking me for him. Kind of flattered, too.

I was grinning wide by then. I stuck out my hand. "Howdy, Josiah. I'm your half brother, Junior by name."

"And by the order of birth, too," Patrick added, kind of snooty.

"And where do you fit in?" Josiah asked Patrick.

"In the middle, of course," Patrick said.

"Of course," said Josiah, although he gave his head a slow shake. Then he turned toward me. "Let's go someplace and palaver. Don't see how I'll ever be shed of you two otherwise."

Well, Josiah ended up tagging along with us, too, and I can't say I was sorry. He was real interesting, Josiah was. Turned out he knew about this Lannigan fellow, too. He must've been famous or something. Not Josiah. I mean Lannigan.

While we rode west, back over to Nevada, I regaled Josiah with stories about Wyatt Earp and Doc Holliday, and he told tales his mama had told him, about running off from her master back in Louisiana and getting to Colorado with a wagon train. He said she did laundry to pay her way, and when they came to Possum Creek, she stayed.

He also insisted that "Possum Creek" was spelled "Opossum Creek," said the *O* was silent. I told him I never heard of such foolishness in my life.

He said my life hadn't been that long yet.

Since he was nineteen and three years my senior, I didn't force the issue. Just as well, because after I read some more books—and got my hands on a dictionary—I found out he was right about the "o."

I also found out you can't count on the English language for making any sense at all.

Still, I kept up my studies. There wasn't a town we rode through that didn't have a few books for sale, although sometimes the pickings were fair slim.

Anyway, Josiah allowed that his mama had worked for a time as a soiled dove, just like Patrick's and mine. He had a tiny painting of her, done by a traveling artist, that he had put in a golden frame with a lid like a pocket watch, and he carried it with him all the time. She was beautiful, all right, and I sort of felt proud of Daddy for having good taste in all his whores.

It was a funny thing to be proud of, but that's what I felt.

His mama's name had been Sophia Washington, he told me, and she had died when he was younger than me. Smallpox. I told him I was sorry.

"At least I had her for fifteen years," he said around the cigar he was lighting. He smoked long, thin, black ready-mades, and he made quite a picture, like a character out of a story. "She was a good woman, and I'm not just sayin' that because she was my ma."

"Oh, sure," Patrick muttered. He was across the campfire from me and Josiah, and we were camped on the Nevada desert.

"Oh, hush your face," I said.

"I'll keep my damned face any way I want to," he snapped.

"If you fellers are done bickerin', I'd appreciate a cup of coffee," said a whole new voice. I'm here to tell you I about jumped out of my skin!

Josiah stood up and said, "Ride in, and welcome."

"What?!" Patrick hissed.

The horsebacker didn't hear him, though. He heard only Josiah's invite, and he rode forward. He dismounted outside the campfire's ring of light and walked up into it.

6

And that's how we met our brother Franklin. He stopped and stared and we did, too, for nigh onto five whole minutes. Unlike the rest of us, he looked to be all white. His hair was dark brown, not black, and wavy, not curly or straight, and he looked to have either regular green or hazel eyes.

At long last, his horse, a steel gray gelding, took a step and moved up to nose him. He put his hand on the horse's neck and said, "Toad, ol' feller, you seein' what I'm seein'?"

The horse bobbed his head a little and I said, "I think that means yes." I stepped toward him and stuck out my hand. "My name's Junior Doyle. This is my brother Patrick, and my half brother, Josiah . . ."

"Josiah Washington," Josiah said with a tip of his hat and a look of pure wonder on his face. He shook hands with the new one right after me.

"If this isn't the damnedest thing! My name's Franklin Hopkins," he said, after he finished shaking hands with Josiah. "The damnedest thing I ever did hear of! You all sons of one Paddy Doyle?"

"We are," Patrick said wearily from his place on the ground. He hadn't got up at all.

"And you been together all these years?"

"More like days," Josiah replied.

"Yeah," Patrick said, then pointed an accusing finger at me. "It was him that done it. Dug us up, I mean."

"Were you buried?"

This was lost on Patrick, but Josiah and I busted out laughing. "Nigh on near, Franklin," Josiah said, once he caught his breath. "Settle your horse in, unpack your bedroll, then come sit down for coffee and a long talk."

"We've got vittles, too, iffen you ain't et yet," I added, and Josiah gave a nod.

"Seems like this is a good crew to run into," Franklin said happily as he led his horse over to the picket line.

"So, you boys on the dodge from somethin' or other?" Franklin asked, his mouth full of leftover fried ham and biscuits. There was just enough to make him a fat sandwich, and plenty of coffee.

"On the dodge?" I asked, although the others seemed to figure right off what he was talking about.

"On the dodge. Runnin' from the law." I must have still looked pretty damned dumb, because he added, "You know, are you bank robbers? Did you kill anybody or anything like that?"

Patrick said, "No, but I been thinkin' about it a lot lately." He was looking square at me when he said it, too.

"How 'bout you, Franklin?" Josiah asked while he poured himself another cup of coffee. "Have you been up to any murderous acts, malicious mayhem, or grandiose thieveries?"

Josiah used five-dollar words like they only cost a nickel. I admit that I admired him for it.

"Not yet," replied Franklin. "Although I wouldn't be opposed to it, iffen I had a chance."

I guess I was kind of shocked, but the statement seemed to have grabbed hold of Patrick's attention. He asked, "You got anything particular in mind?"

Franklin shrugged. "Not yet. Not in particular. But I got this itch to do me somethin' wild, you know, boys?"

Both Patrick and Josiah nodded. I just felt sick to my stomach. I had felt that way once, when I was a big fan of Doc Holliday's, but I guess meeting Wyatt had sunk in deeper and taken wider root than I'd thought.

I said, "You ain't plannin' to do it anytime soon, are you?"

"Not right this second," Franklin said. "Unless you got an idea."

I shook my head no, and—thank God—so did Patrick and Josiah. It seemed like a good time to change subjects, so I asked, "Franklin, how was your mama called by?"

"Emmy Lou Hopkins Doyle," he said without so much as a blink. "Still is, too. Why?"

"Just wondered," I said. "I ain't never had a mama till a couple weeks ago. Patrick's had her all to himself from the beginning."

Patrick grunted, but didn't say anything.

"Mine's kicked, too," volunteered Josiah. "Miss Sophia Washington, by name, from Boulder Grove, Colorado. She was a whore, mostly. Later on, she took in laundry. I got me a half brother by the name of Lincoln Washington. He's older, lives up around Denver. Then there's my little half brother, Jed. He run off when he was younger than you, Junior."

When nobody said a word, Josiah added quickly, "We all got different daddies, of course. Me and my Washington kin, that is."

Patrick smiled just a tad and said, "Bet you're the best-lookin' of any of 'em, ain't you, there, Josiah?"

Josiah leaned back, rested his arms on his knees, and said, "Damn right."

I couldn't help laughing.

Since Josiah and Franklin both said as how Daddy had come from Abilene, Kansas, before he turned up in Nevada, we turned our horses around the next morning and proceeded to start the long trip east.

"This is gonna be nothin' but mountains, mountains, and more mountains," Patrick complained.

I had found myself a geography book back in Possum Creek, and with some sense of authority I said, "No, it ain't. I got a map. Some mountains, but a lot of flat, too."

Patrick turned in his saddle and was about to chew me out, but Josiah stopped him. "Junior's right. I saw a map of the whole U. S. of A., and it's just what he says. These mountains we're just starting up into right now, they'll get smaller, then go away entire. I don't mean they'll really go away. They won't get up and move or anything. But—"

"Yeah, yeah," said Patrick, and reined his horse over to the side, so as to ride alone for a while.

Josiah, who was beside me by then, said, "Cranky sonofabitch, isn't he?"

I nodded. "He likes to be right, I reckon."

"Only child."

I shrugged. "So am I. So's Franklin. At least, I guess he is."

"I don't believe Franklin ever said one way or the other," Josiah opined. He twisted in his saddle: "Hey, Franklin?"

Dust rose and hooves quickened as Franklin

trotted up next to us, to the other side of Josiah. The wind was coming from behind us, so his dust arrived right after he did.

Josiah said, "Say, Franklin, you never told us if you had any brothers or sisters. You got any, or were you an only child?"

"I was . . . You really want to know the whole of it?" Franklin asked.

"Sure!" I said, and Josiah nodded.

"I ain't never told nobody before, but what with runnin' headlong into you boys . . . It's like this."

Franklin proceeded to tell us how his mama, the youngest of three farm girls, had gone and got herself pregnant by our daddy, at which point her papa had tossed her out. She took a horse from his corral and rode after Daddy, he being long gone at the time, until she found him mining silver in some little Nevada town.

I don't know how, and neither did Franklin, but she got Daddy to promise that he'd live with her and call her his wife until after the baby was born. Therefore, Franklin got his "Doyle" legal-like (well, sort of) and Franklin's mama got to live a respectable life, aside from being a grass widow. In those days, that's what they called ladies whose husbands had run off on them. It wasn't legal, but it was better than turning to whoring.

"Suppose that makes you think you're better

than us," snarled Patrick, who had ridden closer without anybody noticing.

"Pardon?" said Franklin.

"Hopkins. What's that? English? We got a nigger and a squaw for mothers."

I never saw any person look like Franklin did just then. He didn't say a word, though.

But Josiah said, "Be careful who you're callin' nigger, Patrick."

Patrick got that snarly look again and started in, "I'll call whoever I want *what* I want, iffen I reckon it's true."

Josiah gathered his reins a little. "A man who ain't careful with his words is liable to wake up dead, I've heard." He kept his voice flat, and his face held no expression. He just looked straight ahead, between his horse's ears.

But I saw his thumb brush back the coattail where it overhung his pistol, and my blood turned to ice water, direct from the Rocky Mountain runoff. I had no way of knowing just how good or bad Josiah was with a handgun, and no wish to find out. At least, not today.

Well, Patrick proved to me that he was smarter in his brain than his mouth when he abruptly dropped the whole subject. I don't know if he glimpsed the movement of Josiah's hand or if he was thinking that he didn't know whose side me or Franklin would be on, or if he actually took Josiah's words to heart.

The point is, he stopped talking. Left the subject behind us in the dust, I guess.

I wanted to point out that our maternal grandpa had been a Frenchman, but I had the sense not to stoke the fire. And I wondered if the next brother or sister we found would turn out to be half Chinese or Mexican or Cajun. It apparently hadn't mattered a whit to Daddy, as long as he thought she was pretty.

Or at least willing.

To tell you the truth, I was beginning to wonder a little about Daddy's moral fiber.

Slowly but with purpose, we kept making our way toward Kansas City.

For the most part, we ate what we could shoot, or what berries we found, or what edible tubers or greens were to be had. I wasn't much good with bringing down game, as I was the only one of us without a rifle, but both Josiah and Franklin proved themselves good marksmen with a long gun. Patrick I still didn't know about, as he had gone sullen—more sullen than usual, at any rate—and wouldn't so much as take a shot at anything. I noticed that he ate good when somebody else brought home the bacon, though.

By the time we got to the Kansas prairie, we were pretty much confined to rabbits and the corn we stole from farmers' fields. There were some nights I would have given my soul for some good old salt and butter, I can tell you that! We did take down one whitetail deer in Kansas, but just one.

When we rode into Abilene, we were all sort of skinny—knees and elbows everywhere, even Josiah, who had started out pretty much like a bull. We had no luck finding anybody who knew of Daddy on the first go-round, and we met up, as planned, at the Good Eats Café for some grub. Me and Franklin were the only ones with any money, so we paid for everything.

Actually, I figured that Franklin should have paid for everything, if only as a way of making amends. He had confided that he'd got his roll from robbing a stage out by Carson City. I admit to being impressed that he'd done it single-handed, but not—like Josiah and Patrick—that he'd done it at all. It didn't even have a payroll on it. He just plucked the passengers' purses.

Even for a onetime robber-in-the-making like me, that fact was enough to turn my stomach. Even Doc wouldn't do such a thing, I figured. Doc would check the stage schedule first and wait for a big haul, like a gold shipment or a government payroll.

'Course, Doc probably wasn't a stage robber, anyway, even though I'd heard he'd been charged with robbing one down in Tombstone. The Earps had investigated and found he had

an airtight alibi—his girlfriend, Big Nose Kate.
No, he liked to rob people legal, in plain sight,
over a poker table.

But those brothers of mine had me a tad worried. They were like I was before I started hanging around with Doc and Wyatt—they were out
after raising a little hell, just to see what it felt
like. In fact, several times over the past weeks I
had come to the fire at night only to find them
huddled in conversation that stopped immediately upon their notice of me.

I never said a word, but I was secretly afraid
they had bad intentions. Not toward me spe-
cifically, but toward the world in general.

In fact, later that very night, after we had
eaten and checked in at one of the local hotels,
I woke in the dark, hard middle of the night to
find them gone. All three of them. At first, all I
could think of was stealing Franklin's bed, except then I remembered he said it had a few
ticks in it. Only when I shuddered did I realize
it was strange that they were all gone at the
same time. There were a couple of thunder jars
in the room, so they wouldn't have all gone to
the outhouse together.

I sat up in my blankets, listening. There were
no sounds, other than the whistle of wind outside and the faint music from a couple of
saloons.

Well, that was it, I decided. They had all gone

off to a whorehouse and left me here! Franklin, who was too cheap to pay for my steak dinner, was treating my brothers to a night on the town, complete with female companionship, and had left me here all by myself.

Oh, I bet they were all having a laugh about that!

So I just lay back down on the floor, madder than a hive full of hornets tossed in the creek! I'd never find them if I looked all night, and they knew it. Oh, they thought they were pretty damned smart, didn't they?

7

Now before I get any further, I think I ought to tell what I had learned about my family so far. We all bore an uncanny resemblance—you already know that. But our upbringing was surely different, one to the next, as a pine tree is to a wild cherry.

Take Patrick. 'Course, that night I would have gladly given him to anyone who asked, on account of he had been so dang surly and hard to get along with for the whole ride.

Even all these years later, I still agree with that decision. It would have saved him a lot of pain and upheaval later on, that's for certain.

Patrick and me, having the same ma, looked the most alike, but were opposite in every other way. Not just reading, I mean, for I loved it while it bored him. And as much as I hate to say it, he was lazy. Now, I was up first most every morning on the trail and, nine times out of ten, had a fire going and coffee brewing and my face washed (and, for what little it was worth in those days, shaved) before he managed to stumble a few feet from his bedroll to make water. Sometimes he had a hard time even making it that few feet.

He was not good with horses. It was several days after our first meeting that I finally had to ask the name of his horse. "Baywing," he said, like he was surprised anybody'd bother to know such a small thing. "Like the hawk." And then he turned back to whittling, and that was that.

I figured Mama must have named it.

And that was another thing. He never would let me get away with calling my mama "my mama" or even "our mama." It was like he wanted to keep her all to himself. I always fought him on this point, though. I figured I had shared our daddy with him, and it was only right he shared our mama.

Of course, I was sharing Daddy with the lot of them, but they were sharing him with me, too. They all knew different stories that their mamas had told them about the olden times and Daddy. And they were all real fascinating. My main point of interest, you can probably guess, was about the days in New York, when he was running with that gang in Five Points.

I had a hard time picturing any sort of a

"gang" in New York City. Did they dress like the outlaws I had seen, or did they favor back-east suits? And that was just question number one.

Josiah was steady in always calling it Five Points, but Franklin called it the Bowery half the time. I would have liked to know which one was proper. I also would have liked to know how Daddy got mixed up in one of these gangs, and what made him leave them and come out west.

I finally decided that he must have crossed the gang somehow, maybe turned them in to the law. I liked to think that was what had happened. I liked to think that Daddy'd had him one of those epiphanies, like me.

If those ran in the family, I can honestly say that my brothers hadn't had theirs yet, nor could I have said with any certainty that they would.

And just what was Five Points, anyway? I think I had it in my mind that it was sort of like Tombstone's tent city—a part of the town but set apart by lawlessness as well as geography, mayhap as little as the width of a street. None of the others seemed to know anything more about it, either, so I had to just let the notion rest.

Josiah did say he'd heard that there was a big riot there around the Civil War times. That would have been just before Daddy left. I don't know what they rioted about for sure, although it probably had something to do with the War, but he talked like it had been a famous thing.

I secretly vowed to get me a history book.

Franklin, like I've said before, was an admitted thief. It just amazed me how many stories he had to tell, how many petty thieveries he'd done, what joy he took in telling the boys all about them, and especially the way they all looked up to him for it. Nobody looked up to me. I was the youngest, for one thing, and I didn't fall down in an apoplexy of pure admiration every time Franklin remembered somebody else he'd flimflammed out of a quarter.

I'm sorry to say it, but I didn't much like Franklin.

Now, Josiah was the brother I liked the best. He irked me sometimes, though. I mean, he was as impressed as Patrick was with Franklin's stories of larceny and all that, but he seemed to like me. At least, he didn't ride me for liking my horse or reading or trying to better myself as best I could.

Josiah was good with cards, too. Maybe he reminded me a little of Doc Holliday, or at least, the part of Doc I admired. Many's the night we whiled away the hours under the starlight by playing games of chance—usually for matches, since the most of us didn't have any money at all.

And Josiah was something, all right. He knew

all the games and all the rules, and he was lucky as sin.

Good, too.

'Course, I knew a good bit about cards and card games, too, having worked for Wyatt at his saloon. But "lucky" wasn't something that was in my natural vocabulary. I was average, at best, at stud and draw, and worse than most at faro. Even Wyatt himself—who dealt it some nights at the Oriental—said that only a fool tries to buck the tiger (that meaning faro) because the odds are always with the house. He said that about roulette, too.

I was hoping that once we reached Abilene, Josiah would pack back on some of that muscle and mass he had displayed when we first started riding together. Not that he looked so awful, but he'd probably lost thirty pounds between Nevada and Kansas. He was also coughing quite a bit of late. He always said it was nothing, and to never mind, but I noticed blood in his handkerchief sometimes.

Doc had the consumption, and there was blood in his handkerchief, too. I didn't want sickness to take a half brother that I'd just got.

Of course, Doc drank real heavy, and I once overheard Wyatt talking with his brother, Virgil, and saying as how the liquor was going to kill Doc one day. I had a feeling that it was the liquor combined with the consumption, because

Wyatt didn't hold himself back any when they were pouring the whiskey or beer.

So maybe just regular meals would get Josiah well. I never talked to him about it. I didn't like to be too pushy, seeing as how he was kind of private-like. For instance, he was open about his mama and brothers, but that was about all. We had no clue as to what he did to make a living before we came across him, or if he had a girlfriend, which was the opposite of Franklin—according to him, he had a girl in every town in Nevada and half of Colorado.

We knew that Josiah was nineteen and rode a bay mare named Hooker, and that he was lucky with cards, and that was about it.

On our second day in Abilene, fortune looked our way. We didn't set out searching until noon, the other boys being beat down from their gallivanting the night before, but I got them up and whipped into shape, and finally up to what we'd come to town for.

It was me who found the clue, if not another sibling. At about four o'clock, I was running out of places to inquire when it suddenly came to me to go to the sheriff's office.

"Oh, sure," said the man behind the desk. I don't think he was the real sheriff, because he wore no badge and he kind of looked out the window before he took a seat behind the desk.

But if he remembered, I didn't care if he just swept the place out. "Paddy Doyle. By God, you look like a younger version of him, all right!"

"So, you recall him passin' through?" I asked, all leaning forward in my chair.

"He was here most of a year, as I recall," said the man. "Hardly call that passin' through." He gave another furtive glance out the window.

"Was there a lady?" I asked. "I mean, one he was extra fond of?" I had come too far to be more subtle than that.

"Josiah!" I shouted. He was just coming up the sidewalk from a saloon. He looked tired, and seemed to be coughing more than usual. But he lifted a hand in answer to my call and came toward me.

For my part, I set off toward him at a run and all smiles. "Colorado!" I practically screamed when I caught him up. "They're back in Colorado!"

"Who?" he asked as he peeled me off him. "Another brother?"

"Mayhap!" I answered. "Daddy was here for nigh on a year. He was keepin' company with a gal called Katheryn Culhane. When he left, she left about a month after, lookin' in a family way. Her sister said she was headed for Spud City, Colorado."

Josiah's face kind of wadded up, and he asked, "Who told you this, Junior?"

"A man up at the sheriff's office." I turned and pointed. "You want to come up and ask him yourself?"

"No, I'll take your word for it. Where the hell's Spud City, anyhow?" He turned, and we began to walk back to the hotel where our room was.

"Not that far," I said, still excited. "The man drew me a map."

"Let's see."

I handed over the old Wanted poster (it was for one "Widow Maker Magee" for the crimes of stage robbery and murder at the posted price of two thousand dollars) the man had drawn on the back of, and Josiah studied on this for a while. On the map, I mean.

"Reckon it's doable," he said. "There's Franklin."

He hollered up Franklin and shared the news, then the three of us went two doors down to the café. Brother-finding is hungry work, I can tell you.

Already I was wondering if we'd find another brother, or maybe a sister this time.

Patrick had beat us to the café and was asleep at a back table, head in his hands. We went back and woke him, but he was so dead asleep that I wondered if he'd been there since the rest of us left at noon. At least, it took him a few minutes to actually hear what we were telling him, like he was pulling himself away from another conversation entirely to speak with us.

And then he said, "Aw, Colorado *again*?" like somebody had just asked him to ride to Mexico City.

At least Franklin was the one to holler at him this time. Patrick never would pay any attention to me.

And by the time Franklin had finished up, Patrick was happy (also fully awake) and I had ordered big bowls of beef stew all around.

With fresh enthusiasm, we set out again the next morning, retracing our steps to the west and wondering what—and who—we would find in Spud City.

8

Going back to Colorado took longer than riding out from it, mainly because it was coming on winter. There was more game that we had better luck taking down, for some reason, but nights were cold enough to freeze the balls off a brass monkey.

Halfway across Kansas, we had a terrible deep snow, too. We couldn't travel at all for three days on account of its howling, driving force, and once we did move on, Consternation fell down a sharp slope and into a hidden creek. Patrick and Franklin thought that was real dang funny, but I spent the next week leading my gimpy Consternation through the waist-high snow.

Josiah let me ride double for some of the time. He said he once found a rattler frozen in midstrike. I didn't like to say anything, but I had a hard time swallowing that.

While I was trudging through that cold, high snow, I got to thinking about Ruby Tulayne and how nice she'd been and how proud she'd be of my reading and writing progress. I was still reading everything I could wrap my eyes around, and practicing my penmanship almost every night in these big yellow tablets I had bought early on.

And then, somehow, I got to thinking about Lannigan, the shootist from Five Points who had probably killed our daddy. I wondered where he was right that minute. He wasn't freezing his feet off, I would have bet. In fact, I'd have bet he was holed up somewhere warm with a soiled dove straddling his lap and a bottle of whiskey at his side.

I hated him like I'd never hated anybody or anything before. Or since, as a matter of fact.

"Doin' it again, aren't you?" Josiah asked me.

"Doin' what?"

"Thinking about it," he said. "The day he died."

"More like who killed him," I said, and tripped over a snow-covered branch.

I scrambled fast to keep from losing my feet altogether, and Josiah held a gloved hand down to me. "Step up, brother, before you murder yourself."

I did, and was grateful for his offer. I couldn't feel my feet anymore.

"You know what my mama used to say to

me, Junior?" he asked, once we got moving again.

I didn't really care at that point, but I said, "What?" just to be polite.

"Doesn't pay to hang on to old hates," said Josiah. And that was all. Frankly, I was expecting something with more wisdom.

"Is there any more?" I asked after a spell.

"Should there be?"

I shrugged, but being in front of me, he didn't see. And he didn't say any more.

The melt started the next afternoon, which made for sloggy going. But it froze that night, leaving us with knee-high crusty snow to plow through the next morning.

Franklin and Patrick had got real testy when the cold snap set in, and they were no better the morning after.

"I never seen such landscape for travelin'!" Franklin said for the fifth or sixth time. I hadn't, either, but at least I had the sense to keep my mouth shut. Every time I'd tried to open my mouth before, my lips had frozen before I got the first syllable out.

"You ain't just foolin'," Patrick replied to him, also for the fifth or sixth time. "Colder out here than a witch's tit!"

Josiah suddenly shot out one arm, pointing. "Smoke!"

I followed his arm, and sure enough, there it

was, far off in the distance: a thin line of smoke, like from a chimney.

"Suppose they could stand some company for the night?" I asked, and was immediately sorry. My lips were half frozen, and the tip of my tongue, too. I sucked it back in fast, to warm it on the back of my bottom teeth.

Franklin and Patrick, in the lead, reined their mounts toward the line of smoke, and Josiah and I followed. The two in the front were laughing, and Josiah called, "What's so funny?" which I would have, except I didn't wish to freeze my mouth all over again.

Franklin swung around in his saddle and shouted back, "Pat says maybe they got a fat smokehouse or like to play cards!"

I made a face, but Josiah laughed and called, "Oh, sure, Franklin, like you'd know what to do! You'll be lucky if they got a friendly daughter."

This time, the three of them all laughed together. I was kind of embarrassed for them. And ashamed of myself, just for thinking about what they were thinking. I hoped those folk up ahead had neither a smokehouse nor a daughter, and I sure hoped they didn't play cards. I'd seen Josiah in action.

It wasn't that he cheated. It was just that he was too good for his own health. Some places, they'd hang a colored man just for being colored. Even part colored. I hated to think what they'd do if he was handy with a deck of cards, too.

Martin Boudreaux was—or had been—a trapper and didn't have a wife, let alone a daughter. Lucky for him, he didn't have a smokehouse, fat or otherwise, and not so much as a faded deck of pasteboards. He had to have been seventy years old, and lived all alone in that godforsaken cabin at the edge of the woods.

He was a colored man, with hands like gnarled walnuts and the face of an apple doll, and he seemed delighted to see us.

"By God, of course you can stay the night!" he cried, arms thrown wide, when Josiah asked him. "Stay the week! Stay as long as you like! Well, stay until that pronghorn I shot yesterday is et up, anyhow. Go on, go on, put your horses up and come back to the house!" he added, once he'd looked us over good. And then, grinning, he slammed the door between him and us, leaving us standing in his front yard.

We made our way to his barn, which was caving in on itself in slow but steady decay. Patrick put his hand on the latch and asked, "You s'pose she'll fall in if I open the door?"

Josiah grinned. "I wouldn't be betting against it."

"Me neither," muttered Franklin, and took a step backward.

But Patrick opened it anyway, banging it back against the frozen snow until he finally got it open wide enough for a horse to pass through. One by one, we led our mounts inside.

The inside wasn't any warmer than the outside, but I figured the horses' body temperature would fix that soon enough. Once my eyes got used to the dim light, I saw that there was a lone horse, sorrel and blanketed against the cold, standing in a back stall. It whickered at our horses as we stripped them of tack.

The building wasn't very big, but there was room for our mounts and tack and such, and still plenty of room for stacks of what looked like old stretchers, frames that had once held drying hides from muskrat-sized to grizzly bear. Martin Boudreaux must have been quite the trapper in his day. I wondered if he had known Mama's daddy, them both being in the same business and all.

After we fed and watered the livestock, we crunched our way back to the cabin with our pack rolls clamped under our arms. There was no telling how good that cabin was sealed, or just how cold it'd get at night.

Mr. Boudreaux greeted us and ushered us into a warm room, though, already smelling of salty pronghorn stew and baking biscuits. We shucked out of our coats and scarves, which he hung around the outside of the hearth, and then he said, "Sit down, boys! I didn't realize you was so young when you was all wrapped up like that." I think he meant our mufflers. "Grab you a seat wherever you can."

He sure was a chatty old goat. He talked and talked and talked, like he hadn't seen a living soul for years, whilst he dished up our suppers. Later on, he insisted we have a Bible reading, which he was glad to provide.

I admit to being bored, but tried not to show it. Not so Patrick. He said, "Aw, I ain't gonna listen to this crud," and went out into the freezing weather, talking to himself.

He slept in the barn, too, out of his own choosing.

Now, I don't like to gripe about folks, but I had about had it with my only full brother. A person would think it was no more than polite to listen to a few Bible verses, even if he didn't believe in God, from a man who had just fed you good and promised you shelter for the night.

Back then, I don't know why Patrick did it. I thought maybe he was just showing off for the others. Maybe he was just crazy. I knew Ma hadn't raised him to be that way.

'Course, what did I really know about my ma? Maybe she had brought him up to believe in the Crow gods instead of the real one.

I doubted it, though.

Josiah listened attentively, or at least seemed to, and Franklin fell asleep. Well, maybe he just pretended to. But eventually, Martin Boudreaux gave up on us and we lapsed into conversation.

"Pardon me, Mr. Boudreaux, but I saw a lot of those old hide-stretchers out in the barn," I said. "You must have been a whip-crack trapper, back in the day."

"That I was, boy, that I was!" He took out a jug and pulled the cork free with his teeth. "Care for a blast?" he asked, offering it.

I shook my head.

He shrugged and had himself a long pull before offering it to Josiah, who gladly accepted. He broke out in a fit of coughing directly after he swallowed, and his face got all screwed up. "Smooth," he said hoarsely as he passed it back.

Boudreaux grinned. "That she is, son." He turned back toward me and said, "Why, when I first come west, it weren't all crammed full of white folks. Just Injuns and beaver and grizzers and the like. Made pals with most of the Injuns, and skinned the critters. Now?" he asked, pausing. "Now the beavers is gone, even the grizzers and the minks. A few fox and every once in a while, a wolf or two, but not like the old days, no, sir. It's enough to make an old man quit trappin'."

A smile crossed his lips before he hiccuped through a laugh. "Guess it has, hasn't it? Made me quit, I mean."

"How do you get by, then?" asked Josiah, whose voice had returned to normal.

"Oh, I got me some saved by," Boudreaux replied with a wink.

That roused Franklin. "Are we done with Leviticus?" he asked sleepily, rubbing his eyes.

"Yes, and you're missin' out on some interesting conversation, Frank," Josiah said.

All of a sudden I had a real bad feeling.

9

I should have took that feeling more serious, because several days later, after we had found out we were in Colorado already and had turned northwest toward our goal, Franklin couldn't stand it anymore and he flashed his wad—a roll of bills as big as my fist. It had been as big around as my thumb when we left Abilene.

"Franklin, what did you do?" I asked, even though I knew the answer.

"I found his money hole," he said, and threw me a wink. "At least, the one with the folding money in it. It was in a little cubbyhole out in the barn, and I mean, how stupid can you get? I didn't have time to find the one with the coins, more's the pity."

This made me just about boil over. Real stern, I said, "Franklin, you can't go around stealing an old man's money! That was most likely all he had for the rest of his life!"

Franklin tucked the roll back in his pocket and shrugged. "So what?"

"So what? That's just plain mean, that's so what!"

Patrick had let his horse drift back, and now he asked, "What you two goin' on about?"

"Franklin stole Mr. Boudreaux's retirement money!" I said, all full of umbrage and superiority.

Patrick's face lit up like Christmas. "Hey, good goin', Frank! Now, what are you so fired up about, Junior?"

"But it was his retirement money! He fed us and gave us a warm place to sleep, and—"

My jaw clamped up on me and I stopped talking. They had loped on ahead to join Josiah, anyway.

That night, after we were camped, Patrick asked Franklin to show him the money. He whistled at the size of the roll and Josiah made an agreeable sound while Franklin counted it out. "Two thousand and some," he said with a smile so smarmy I wanted to slap it off his face.

"By jingo!" cried Patrick, and slapped his knee.

"You get it all, Frank?" Josiah asked. "You clean him out?" I could tell he was conflicted, although I had no idea whether it was because

Mr. Boudreaux was another colored man, like him, or whether he didn't think it was nice to take somebody's life savings.

I didn't get to find out right away, because Franklin didn't answer him. Instead, he re-pocketed the bills, saying, "I reckon we'll pull into Spud City tomorrow afternoon. And when we do, I'm buying steak dinners all around!"

Patrick let out a hoot, and I just looked down at my boots. I couldn't see Josiah's face, but I was downright ashamed to admit that the other two were any kin of mine. I made a silent vow to pay Mr. Boudreaux back every cent that Franklin had stole off him, even though I didn't have more than a dollar and eighteen cents to my name. That's the confidence of youth for you, I guess.

'Course, I did get him paid back—and was damned glad to get rid of the money, too—but that's for later in the story.

Anyway, I guess I wasn't good company for the rest of the night. I just sat off from the others and didn't speak one word unless I was spoke to first.

Which wasn't much.

We rode into Spud City at about five o'clock, and Franklin was true to his word. We all had pound-and-a-half steaks, with fried potatoes and peas and onions and biscuits and honey on the side. I can't say I felt too fine about eating it, seeing as it was Mr. Boudreaux really paying for it, but I hogged mine down the same as everybody else. It was awful good.

After, we all had dried-apple pie with cheddar cheese, and Franklin started talking.

"What's the name of this lady we're supposed to find again?" he asked me.

"Katheryn Culhane. Can't you remember anything?" I was feeling a little moody at the moment, about Mr. Boudreaux.

Franklin looked at me sort of queer, and then turned to Patrick. "I reckon it's too late to look tonight, don't you think, Pat?"

"Yup," Patrick said around a mouthful of pie. "It's come dark. Might try the saloon, though. Weren't none of Daddy's women too clean-cut." And then he laughed, and Franklin joined in with him.

I'd about had it. I stood right up. I stood up so fast that I knocked my chair over backward. "You shut up, Patrick. That's my ma you're talkin' about."

He slouched in his chair like he didn't have a care in the world. "So what? Mine, too." And then he leaned forward and put his hands flat on the table. "Listen, Junior, you don't know nothing about it. You wasn't the one livin' behind a saloon all them years. You wasn't the one listenin' to Ma and her 'friends' carryin' on in the next room. You wasn't the one raised up by whores and their drunkards. No, you had our big fine daddy, had him all to yourself for sixteen years. And don't tell me he didn't get all the bitches in Tombstone in whelp, too. You can't teach an old dog new tricks, and you can't break him of bad habits, neither."

Now, this was the most, all in a row, that Patrick had ever said to me, and I was practically dumbfounded. I mean, he talked to himself a lot, but not to me.

I think I stood there for a minute with my jaw lying slack on my chest before I finally mustered, "Daddy never had another woman. He slept every night in the same shack as me."

But Patrick ignored me. He had got back to his pie, and to whispering with Franklin. Josiah put his hand on my arm, and I sat down again, after I righted the chair.

"Don't pay him any mind," Josiah said, soft so only I could hear. "We've all got the same daddy, and we all got our feelings 'bout him. Guess it's hard for you and Patrick, sharing both mama and papa, only seein' things from opposite sides of the fence, you know?"

"I suppose," I said, picking up my fork. "It's just that he can't seem to make up his mind about Mama. And he never takes Daddy's side."

"Some people are just confused," Josiah said, like it was sage advice. I didn't see it, though.

I took a bite of my pie and was silent for the rest of the evening.

I didn't even go to the saloon with them.

It was after midnight when they came back to the hotel room, all arguing and rowdy and cussing, and turning up lamps and lighting candles. It woke me straight up.

"What?" I said, rubbing my eyes. "What has got you in such an uproar?"

Josiah sat down hard on the edge of one of the beds. He ripped off his hat and ran his hand back over his dark curls and said, "They're gonna hang him, Junior. They're gonna hang him!"

"Hang who?" The only one I thought deserved it was Franklin. Well, Patrick, too, but that was just on general principles. But they were all right there, in the room with us. "Who they goin' to hang, Josiah?"

"Our brother."

I looked from one face to the next. "Which one?"

"Not us, you loon," snarled Franklin. "Our brother Seamus."

My face couldn't help but light up. "We got another one?"

Patrick took an angry step toward me, but Josiah stood up and moved between us. That stopped Patrick, all right. After a minute of glaring at each other, Patrick backed off and Josiah sat on the bed again, only closer to me. He put his hand on my shoulder and said, "Junior, we went to the saloon and asked around about Katheryn Culhane, and a man there said that a fella named Seamus Culhane had shot another man and was gonna hang for it next week."

"And another one there said that Katheryn was his mama, that she'd raised him up in this town," Franklin broke in. "Afore she died."

"So we knew it had to be the right one," muttered Patrick, just to keep his end of the conversation up.

"Did you go see him?" I said. I was feeling all twitchy inside. "Maybe he didn't do it!"

"Well, that'd be pretty damned stupid, wouldn't it? If Daddy stamped true, they'd know us for his brothers right off," said Patrick, real snippy. "They'd probably arrest us, too!"

"Why didn't they know you in the saloon, then?" I said.

Josiah turned his hat in his hands. "Dim lights . . . ?"

"Me and Patrick took a vote, Junior," Franklin said. "You and Josiah're gonna go and see him tomorrow. You know, give him all our last regards, tell him good luck and all that."

I said, "Franklin, I know why you aren't goin'. You thieved that money off Mr. Boudreaux and you're afraid they'll find out and hang you, too. But why's Patrick not goin'?"

I figured that Patrick was just too lazy to be troubled, and since he didn't bother to answer me, I took that for a yes.

"All right," I said to Franklin. "All right with you, Josiah?"

He nodded, like he was as ashamed of Patrick as I was.

Me, I just turned my back on them, snugged up my ratty hotel quilt around my neck and said, "Turn those lights down. I'm tired."

Now, it's one thing to learn that you have got a slew of brothers out there that didn't know about you—or you about them—until just a few months or so ago, but it's another thing entire to learn that one is a downright thief, one's a cantankerous—not to mention crazy—sonofabitch, and one's a gambler.

And still another thing to find out that one's a deadly killer, already tried and judged and awaiting the hangman's noose.

I was beginning to wonder why I hadn't just stayed in Tombstone.

The next morning, I rose early and, without waking the other two, nudged Josiah awake and got to the jail by seven. The town sheriff not being on duty yet, we were met by a drowsy deputy, who let us in, then immediately excused himself to use the outhouse. I guess he'd been drinking coffee all night.

No one else was there except the prisoner, asleep in his bunk, his back to us. I didn't figure it could be a brother of ours. For one thing, he was short. He couldn't have been even six foot, because his feet didn't hang off the end of the cot. And for another, he had reddish blond hair. Those were two things that Daddy had stamped his get with: a towering height and black hair.

But Josiah whispered that we should wake him up anyway.

And so I did. After some mutterings, then some normal talk, and then some shouting, Josiah finally took matters into his own hands and roused him with a poke from a broom handle.

The strawberry blond sat up and turned toward us.

"Well, I'll be jiggered" was the first thing that came out of his mouth, after the yawn.

He was the spitting image of me, only the bleached-out version. He even had light blue eyes like me. But he was about a foot shorter. Maybe five foot and some.

"D-Doyle?" I stammered. "Your papa Paddy Doyle?"

"That he was," came the reply. "I got a feelin' I'm related to the two of you, by the looks of it." A smile tickled at the corners of his mouth.

"That you are, boyo," said Josiah in a sing-song fashion, which was real surprising coming from a colored man. I believe I stared at him.

"Well, what are you waitin' for?" asked Seamus. "Get me out of here before they get a chance to stretch my neck!"

Jailbreak? The idea of it was still crawling across my mind when Josiah had found the keys and was already unlocking the jail door, his head twisting like an owl's while he listened for any sign of the deputy.

"Josiah?" I said. "We can't—"

The cell door swung open and Seamus was on his feet and pushing past me.

Seamus remarked, "Seems Papa was one for scatterin' his seed far and wide," to Josiah.

"You got a horse?" was Josiah's only reply.

"Aye, down to the livery."

"Hurry up, then."

Josiah pushed us out the front door, then took off, running for the hotel to wake the others. Seamus began running for the livery. He was mighty fast, considering how stumpy his legs were. I followed, for the lack of anything better to do.

We raced inside the livery and Seamus went directly to the stall of a black gelding and threw his arms around its neck. "Kilkenny, me old love!" he exclaimed before he went to slinging tack.

I followed suit. I suppose Consternation was a little surprised to see me up and around this early, but he didn't complain, especially when I gave him a handful of oats.

By the time we were mounting, Patrick,

Franklin, and Josiah all shoved through the door
shoulder to shoulder and got right to work sad-
dling their horses.

"Big lot, aren't you?" Seamus said to me.

"Daddy was big."

"Mother was a wee bit of a songbird. Which
way?"

I hadn't opened my mouth when Franklin
shouted, "South, by the bend in the creek! Get
going!"

We did, and galloped out of town far ahead
of our brothers.

10

Me and Seamus pulled up by the bend in the creek long before we spotted the other three on the horizon, and therefore we had time to catch our breath and talk for a few minutes.

The first thing out of my mouth was, in fact, "Where'd you get that blond hair?"

"Mama," he said. "Where'd you get that black mop?"

I blinked. "Daddy, of course."

"Sure," he said. "Like I've ever so much as laid an eye to him."

He had me there. "Your mama, she was Irish?" I half expected to look down and see him wearing those little leprechaun boots instead of regular ones.

"Born and bred. Just like . . . him. 'Cept she wasn't black Irish. Reckon he had some Spaniard in him from the Armada days, if he had black hair."

"What the heck are you talking about?" I wasn't very good at history yet.

He started to tell me but stopped, on account of just then our other three brothers came galloping down the hillside.

"They ain't onto us yet, but we'd best ride like the Denver Flyer, for a while, anyhow," huffed Franklin.

"Deputy musta fell in the outhouse hole." Josiah smirked.

"Who'd you kill, anyhow?" demanded Patrick. "Anybody famous?"

"Sort of," replied Seamus with a funny smile. "Let's go!"

He went first, and we followed him at a lope back through the pass from whence we'd come.

He turned us straight west after a couple of hours, at which point we stopped to rest the horses. I don't know about the others, but Consternation was all in. I stripped his tack off and walked him for a good long spell before I watered and grained him. Not so the others. They just threw their blankets over their mounts and that was it. I suppose they figured they were cooled out enough, since we'd slowed down to a trot for the last mile or two.

I was greeted by Patrick's, "You're too damn good to that nag of yours, Junior," when I joined them at the campfire.

"Shut up," I said. I was so tired my very bones ached.

"A man can't be too good to his horse," Seamus said, although I don't know that it was in my defense. "You'll find yourself afoot one day, and learn it for certain."

Patrick glared at him.

"My goodness, but we all have a similar face," said Seamus. "Don't tell me we're each one of us—"

"Sons of the same careless sonofabitch," said Franklin. "Mr. Paddy Doyle, Senior, by name."

"Even though he wasn't pumpin' up to the full measure with you, Shorty," Patrick said. I couldn't see his face.

"Ain't there nothin' comes out of your mouth that isn't mean, Patrick?" I snapped. Like I said, I was awful beat out, and probably overstepped myself. But I didn't care.

Patrick didn't answer me. He just jumped to his feet in less time than it took me to blink, shoved Josiah aside, and slugged me.

I went flying. 'Course, I wasn't prepared for it, but he was that strong. By the time I had the sense to shake my head and push myself up on my elbows, all hell had broken out. Little Seamus was going after Franklin, who looked to have been going after Josiah, who was presently pounding Patrick into the ground.

I shouted, "Stop it!" before I realized that I

might be calling the whole passel of them down on my head. And even after I realized it, I yelled, "Stop, dang it!" again. That time I got their attention.

"Sorry, Junior," Josiah said after he threw Patrick down. Well, more like dropped him. He came over and put his hand down to me, which I took.

After he hauled me up, I said, "Thank you, Josiah. I figure we're brothers, at least half brothers, and we ought to be civil to each other. Least till we get to know each other. I've known Patrick longer than any of you, and we're brothers all the way through, so maybe my gettin' mad at him can be excused. But it ain't no reason for all five of us to go at it."

"Sorry, Junior," said Seamus, rubbing at his chin. It was swelling up something fierce.

Patrick just grunted and glowered.

Franklin sat down on the ground, put his hat back on, and nodded.

"For the baby of the tribe, you're right smart, Junior," Josiah said, and winked at me. I grinned back.

The rest of us went back to the little fire Seamus had built and sat around it whilst Josiah got the coffeepot and fixings. I said, "The next thing we've gotta do is figure where Daddy was before you were born, Seamus. To see if we got more kin, I mean."

"There's only Doreen," he replied matter-of-factly.

Franklin and I, at the same time, said, "Doreen?"

"She's about two years older than me," Seamus said. "Daddy married her mother, or so she says. She's wed to a preacher. Believe they're out to Oregon now."

Nobody said anything except for Josiah, who was putting the coffee on and cursed softly when he nearly upset the pot on the side of a rock.

"Wed to a *preacher*?" I muttered. I couldn't imagine a sister of any of us would be so upstanding. A soiled dove or an axe murderer would have been more like it.

"Yup," said Seamus, and took one of the empty tin mugs Josiah was handing out.

Josiah, who seemed not very interested in sisters, asked, "So who'd you kill, Seamus? Seeing as me and Junior busted you out, I think we got a right to know."

"Wasn't nobody but a nigger cardsharp," said Seamus, who then remembered who he was talking to. "I mean, it was a colored feller. I think he must have had six aces up his sleeve. Least, three fell on the table. And since I was holdin' the other three, well . . ."

"Sad thing when a man's clumsy with cards," Josiah said. I couldn't read his expression.

"But what about before that?" I said. "I mean before this Doreen, not the card game."

"Before Doreen, our da was in the Bowery, runnin' the finest floatin' craps game west of Tipperary. At least, accordin' to him," Seamus said. "That's what he told my sainted mother, anyhow, and it's what she passed along to me."

We put a few more miles between us and town before we camped for the night, in an old cave that Seamus knew of. We had traveled over some snowless, rocky ground that afternoon, so I was pretty sure that we'd thrown off any posse that Spud City could muster.

The cave was deep and wide and low-ceilinged, but we barely had room to lead our horses through the opening to it. Once we were in, though, there was plenty of room for all of us. I could have stayed there a long time, so long as I had something to read.

I didn't read that night, though, because Seamus let loose with all kinds of tales of our daddy, from his Bowery days until he left Seamus's mother. He even mentioned Lannigan once or twice.

I kept my ears perked. It seemed that Daddy ran a kind of dice game that moved every night, from alley to back room to hotel room and back to the alleys again. That was what Seamus meant by "floating." And he hadn't been a

member of a gang, although he had pissed off
two or three. Seems his craps game floated into
the wrong territory a few times too many, and
he didn't pay "tribute" like he was supposed to.

That was when Lannigan got involved. After
Daddy took off for the West with Doreen's
mother, he heard that Lannigan's boss had sent
Lannigan after him, like a dog on a scent. He'd
told Lannigan not to come back till Daddy
was dead.

I guess either Lannigan had a real mean boss
or at least he thought so, because if he'd held
the rifle that killed my dad, it had taken him
nearly twenty-five years to do it.

Now, that is determination! You almost had
to admire him.

I didn't, though.

Seamus also spoke of Daddy's early mining
efforts in Colorado, how he had prospected on
his own for a while (without much luck) until
he got word of the Comstock Lode, back in the
late 1850s. Then he was off and running.

And procreating all over the West, too, I
suppose.

He kept on with that last part for a good long
time, too.

Well, we voted on whether we should look
up Doreen, and it was the four of them voting
for getting up to some mischief against me,
holding out for Doreen. In the end, they relented

enough that I was able to write her a letter and tell her about her brothers. I addressed it to "Mrs. Remus Skink"—that being her married name, according to Seamus—in care of General Delivery in Spottsville, Oregon, and stuck it in my pocket, intending to send it when we reached somewhere that had a post office.

Now, Seamus had known Doreen most of his life and had even gone to school with her, them living in the same town and all, but he always wondered why there was such bad blood between his mama and hers. When he was eighteen, his mother finally fessed up and told him all about it.

And by then, Doreen was married to a preacher and gone.

He said she was pretty, though, and dark of hair, and a few inches taller than he was. I could understand why the others didn't care to ride clear up to Oregon, but I vowed to one day go see her. After all, she was my own half sister. And having married up with a man of God, she must not have had a criminal bent, like most of her siblings. I figured I'd like her.

Now, I said before that the other fellers voted for getting up to some mischief instead of going to Oregon. Nobody said exactly what they meant by that, so I took it for some general slang, meaning that they just wanted to saddle-tramp it for a while. And I supposed that this was fine by me, too. If they didn't want to go to Doreen's, there was nothing else pressing on me.

I did have my qualms about being seen riding with Seamus, but I figured that once we got far enough away from Spud City it wouldn't make much difference. "Far enough" would be into the next state or territory, seeing as how back then they didn't have all this "extradition" stuff going on like we do now. Most lawmen's authority ended at the city limits.

Somebody might put out a paper on Seamus, but I didn't think it likely that the town would put together a reward of anything over fifty dollars. And according to Seamus, he had killed a drifter with no known kin.

I was anxious to leave Colorado, though, since Franklin's big robbery had taken place there and I had only a vague idea of how much he'd made off with. For all we knew, he could have had the U.S. Marshals out after him.

There was no telling with Franklin, though, no telling with any of them. But they were my brothers, so I figured to tag along for a while. After all, I'd started this whole thing, hadn't I? I supposed it was my duty to see it through to the end.

11

About two months later, we found ourselves in Mirage, California, a place I figured to be about as close as any to a ghost town. There were a few people around, but it was sure headed in that direction. It was in the southern half of the state—across from Arizona instead of Nevada—and Josiah seemed to know some people there.

One of them was a feller about my age. Seth was his name, Seth Winters. He was my favorite of Josiah's friends, anyway, although Patrick and Franklin didn't much care for him. He was shorter than me, about six foot or a little more without his boots, and sandy-haired and green-eyed, and he had a good sense of humor.

We met in a bar, the Yuma Queen by name— even though Yuma, the town, was a good seventy miles farther south—and I didn't get much of a chance to get a word in edgewise at first. Franklin was busy buying us all drinks and plates of food—with Patrick's help, of course— while Josiah was trying to introduce his friends and Seamus was over at the bar trying to make time with the place's lone whore.

Me, I was wondering what our sister, Doreen, would make of all this: two of her brothers squandering an old man's retirement money, while a third tried to show off for a common soiled dove. She wasn't even very pretty, having only one top front tooth. Didn't he know that he only had to show her some money?

Apparently not, because she shook her head at last and watched after him, exasperated, while he made his way back to our table. Seth, who was seated next to me, leaned over and said, "Don't that brother of yours know nothin' about fair trade?"

I laughed. I guess he had been watching Seamus at work, too.

"What's so funny?" Seamus snapped as he yanked out his chair and sat down across from me.

I kept my mouth shut and stared at the table, but Seth said straight out, "She's a workin' girl, Seamus. Don't you know you're supposed to offer her some cash? Or at least a pair of red shoes or a fancy frock for doin' your business with her?"

"I ain't got no money," Seamus growled.

"Well, get a job. Or borrow the money from your rich brother. Franklin, ain't it?"

Franklin, hearing his name spoken, turned briefly toward Seth, then dove back into conversation with Patrick.

Seamus blinked a few times fast, then grumbled and grunted out something I didn't understand. Then he, too, joined in conversation with Patrick and Franklin.

"It's stolen money," I offered softly.

"That true, Josiah?" Seth said to Josiah, who was on the other side of him from me. "Your brother there, a thief?"

Josiah leaned over and whispered something in Seth's ear. Then Seth turned to me and repeated the procedure, saying softly, "Josiah says you'd best keep your braggin' to yourself."

I pulled back to see him grinning at me, but I was kind of mad. I said, "It wasn't no brag. He held up a stage before we met him, and then he stole an old man's life savings. If that don't make him a thief, I don't know what does."

Seth just stared at me for a second, with no emotion showing on his face whatsoever, and then he stood up. "What you say you and me go on down to Mary's Café, Junior?" He bent over and asked Josiah what I figured was the same question, because Josiah stood straight-away.

"But I don't have any money," I whined.

"Get up, kid," Seth said. "I do. And it's better food than the swill you'll get here."

We didn't say a word to the others, who weren't paying attention anyway. We left the saloon and proceeded up the street.

"What'd you wanna travel with trash like that, anyhow, Josiah?" Seth asked as we walked.

"They're my brothers," Josiah said with a shrug.

"They're a bunch of bad-tempered thieves, if you was to ask me," Seth replied through clenched teeth. "Exceptin' Junior, here. You got one of 'em tryin' to talk a workin' girl into givin' it away for nothin', you got one who's a down-and-out thief, and another who's thicker with him than pine sap stuck on a glove in December. I think you got the bad end of the brother stick. That goes for you, too, Junior."

I didn't quite know what to say, but I agreed with him. I nodded at the ground. I don't know what Josiah did, but he didn't say anything that I heard.

"Well, that is sure a sorry tale," Seth said as he dove into his beef stew. He was right about the vittles. They were awful good, but the biscuits were the best. They fried them instead of baking them, and served them up with mesquite honey. They were the best I'd ever had in my life. Haven't yet had better, as a matter of fact.

"But they're our brothers," Josiah said again. He owned a little pocket money, and had spent most of it on a real steak about two inches thick that he had cooked raw in the middle. He said he liked it that way, though I can't think why. It like to turned my stomach, just to see it oozing blood into his potatoes.

"Josiah, I'm sorry," I said all of a sudden. "It was my fool idea to go looking for my ma, and when I did, I found Patrick, too. I don't rightly know what happened. I guess he said 'come on' and I did."

Both Josiah and Seth stared at me.

"He was my big brother," I said, in my defense. When they still didn't say a word, I yelped, "Well, he *was*!"

"Calm down there, Junior." It was Seth. He signaled the waiter—who also seemed to be the cook, table clearer, and floor sweeper, too—that I needed more stew. I had scraped my bowl clean without knowing it.

"It's all right, Junior," Josiah added. "None of us knew that Patrick was gonna be Patrick or Franklin was gonna be Franklin."

"Or that Seamus was gonna be . . ." I said lamely. "Well, yes, we did know that when we busted him out of jail. Stupid thing to do."

"Don't kick yourself, kid," said Josiah. "I was there, too, you know."

Seth said, "I swear, you boys have left me straddlin' a whole heap of questions."

Neither me nor Josiah said a thing, which left Seth to cock a curious brow.

Josiah and I told him what we knew, by which time we had repaired back to the saloon. Josiah said he felt like a little game of cards. Seeing as he only had two dollars and change left from his dinner, I didn't think this was the best idea anybody'd ever come up with, but Seth wasn't worried, so I tagged along.

Seth said he'd known Josiah since Josiah was ten and he was about seven, and Josiah saved him from being beat bloody by a bigger boy. That wasn't a very smart thing for Josiah to do, he said, since this was back in Texas and not long after the War, when lynching coloreds for doing a lot less was common.

Seth took Josiah home with him, and Seth's folks hid Josiah and his whole family for six months until a colored wagon train came through.

He said they met up again in New Mexico a few years back.

"Can't seem to shake the sonofabitch," Josiah said, grinning, then turned to a feller at the only table with a game going to ask if he could sit in.

The feller was agreeable, and that was the last I heard from Josiah for quite a while. Me and Seth sat down at a corner table, had a beer or two, and just talked.

"Them other two boys with me? Rance and Ed?" He nodded up front, where they were still sitting with my three other brothers. "Josiah ain't known 'em long. In fact, he met 'em about ten minutes after I did, down by the livery. Guess he figured since he met us in a bunch, we was saddle companions. Didn't have time to tell him no different."

"Because we were right on his tail," I said, remembering that hole they called a livery. I wondered how Consternation was handling it, then decided that horses probably didn't care what their surroundings looked like. They only cared that they had good food and clean water and deep bedding. All of which I'd seen to before I'd left him.

"So, iffen you don't trust 'em any further than you could pick 'em up and heave 'em, why you still ridin' with 'em? And don't say because they're your brothers."

He had taken away the only reason I could think of, and I didn't answer him.

"I tell you what," he said after he took another swallow of beer. "Why don't me and you and Josiah light out of here tomorrow? Seems to me those brothers of yours are headed straight for the gallows, and I'd hate to see you and Josiah go along for the ride."

Now, being pretty sick of Patrick and Franklin, and to tell the truth, scared of Seamus, I was all for it. I could take Josiah and Seth back to Tombstone and introduce them to Wyatt, and we would all get jobs.

The fact that Ruby Tulayne was in Tombstone held a certain draw, too.

But still I said, "You'd have to talk that over with Josiah." I reckoned Josiah could make a good living gambling down in Tombstone without getting hanged. There were plenty of people there of all colors and races, and they all seemed to get along pretty dang well.

But first he had to decide to go.

"Don't know, Seth," Josiah said three hours later when he quit the game. He had parlayed that two bucks into something over seventy, and decided to get while the getting was still good. "I got three other brothers to consider, you know."

I was real disappointed. I had expected him to jump at the chance. But he walked on over to the others without even sitting down to hear the rest of our—actually, Seth's—reasons, and pulled out a chair next to Patrick.

They talked for quite a long time, long enough for Rance and Ed, Seth's friends, to get antsy enough to belly up to the bar and have a few beers.

We couldn't hear what they were saying, those brothers of mine, but Franklin and Patrick, especially, had a heated tone to their voices, and Seamus kept getting up and then sitting again. "It don't sound too good for our side," I muttered.

Seth nodded. "I got to agree with you there, Junior."

12

Well, Seth and I were right. Our side didn't win. In fact, the three of them joined up with the five of us riding south the next morning. The way we rode indicated the two camps, too. Seamus, Patrick, Franklin, Rance, and Ed all moved along in a tight pack up front, and Josiah, Seth, and I hung back a bit, riding three abreast.

I don't think I have told you what Rance and Ed were like. Rance was tall, Ed a bit shorter, and both had brown hair and brown eyes. Their last name was Sharpe, and I figured them to be brothers, even though they hadn't said as much. They both had roundish faces and real long eyelashes, and only Rance had the first traces of a beard.

They were both good-looking brown-skinned boys, I suppose, but boys was what they were.

Heck, they even made me look half grown-up. 'Course, I didn't have much face hair, either, but I figured it was because I was half Indian.

Patrick was a year my senior, and he didn't have much, either.

We started—or rather, the bunch we were following—swung left, and the three of us did, too. I was afraid they were going to go over into Arizona. I just hoped they'd pick a place like Prescott or Phoenix to end up in. Wyatt wouldn't be happy if I brought them to Tombstone.

Seth broke our long silence by saying, "Almost forgot. Gotcha somethin', Junior."

He fumbled behind him in his saddlebag for a few seconds, and then pulled out a book. He handed it to me.

"Gosh, thanks!" I said before I even looked at it. Nobody had ever given me a present before, unless you counted Miss Ruby Tulayne.

"Aren't you even going to look at it?" asked Josiah, his eyes glinting.

"Sure! Sure!" I said, and turned the book over in my hands. I gasped. Not because it looked like the book had been sitting on the shelf for a couple of years, but because of the title: *The Life and Legend of Spats Lannigan.*

"Lannigan?" I shot a glance toward Josiah. "Our Lannigan?"

"Reckon so," he said. "Read the back cover."

I did.

"Small world, ain't it, Junior?"

"Josiah mentioned somethin' about it last night," said Seth, "and I picked it up on the way out of town." I think my jaw was still hanging open.

"You think it'll do you any good?" Seth asked hopefully.

I guess I nodded. Before, I'd just thought that Lannigan was a man with a grudge against Daddy from a long time ago. It had never crossed my mind that he might be a famous man, a famous killer.

I must've been rude, because I didn't say another word to either Josiah or Seth. I just opened that book and started reading, oblivious to the rest of the world.

If I had hoped to find any references to my daddy, I was pretty disappointed. He was only mentioned twice in the first half of the book— as much as I had read by the time we camped for the night—and was mostly referred to not by his name but as a "scrofulous runner of card games" who had consistently cheated one Mr. William "Boss" Tweed out of his cut in said games of chance.

Lannigan worked as hired muscle for Boss Tweed, and I guessed that Boss Tweed was not one to take a shortfall lightly.

Anyhow, the book was mostly about Five Points—which I found out was bordered on one side by the Bowery, but was not part of it—and Tammany Hall, and Spats Lannigan wasn't in it very much at all. But I guess the publisher needed a title that would sell books.

All in all, it was fair interesting, though. There was lots of back-east slang from before I was born, words I'd heard Daddy use, like "Mort" for a girl and "barking iron" for a gun, and lots more I never heard before, like "rhino" for money. There were others, too, but I couldn't figure them out, not even in the context of the whole.

When Seth laid out his pack roll next to mine and asked if I'd learned anything new about my daddy from the book, I watched Josiah build the fire and had to say, "Not much. But on Five Points in general, I'm gettin' to be quite an expert. And it's Five Points, Franklin, not the Bowery."

Franklin looked up from the prairie chicken he was cleaning. "So? Who told you any different?"

It is one thing to score one on your big brother, and another thing entirely to have him pretend you're crazy. I didn't appreciate it one whit.

"Aw, you did, Franklin," called Josiah. "We all heard you, so don't go pretendin' otherwise." I hadn't even known he was listening.

It was a good thing it was him that called Franklin on it, too. Not that I'm a coward. Don't go thinking that. It's just that Franklin was a lot older and trickier than I was, and Seamus, a convicted killer, was helping him with those prairie hens.

Franklin, according to his nature, stood right up and said, "Say that again, nigger."

This time it was me that shot to my feet, though I don't remember doing it. "You cut that out, Franklin," I said. "You stop callin' Josiah names. He's your brother, too."

And then Josiah was standing next to me with his hand on my shoulder. "Sit down, kid. This is betwixt Franklin and me."

I sat back down on my rock, albeit slowly, and looked back and forth between Franklin and Josiah. Franklin was making signs of backing off already. His fingers twitched a little and he blinked a couple times, fast. He opened his mouth to speak, but Josiah beat him to it.

"What I said, Franklin, was that you been saying Five Points and the Bowery like they're the same place. We all heard you. Did I make myself clear enough to suit you this time?"

Franklin was really getting twitchy now, because Josiah's voice was so steady, deep, and serious. And he wasn't squirmy at all.

Finally, he said, "Yeah, Josiah. Sorry. And I apologize, Junior, if I was mistook. I ain't never been that far east, and I am bad at geography to boot." Then he added, "Sit down, Seamus," in a near frantic hiss, because Seamus was starting to get up, too. I guess Franklin was not too smart, but he had the sense to know he didn't want to get killed by anybody, be it friend, foe, or brother.

He asked, "Are we all right, brother?"

Josiah took his eyes from Seamus and put them back on Franklin. "For now," he said, in a rumbling tone. "Just remember, Junior ain't no dummy. He reads. He reads everything from Wanted posters to the little bitty words on the back of tooth powder boxes. And he's been riding with his nose in that new book about Spats Lannigan all afternoon."

That worried me—being called attention to, I mean—but Josiah sat down and so did Franklin. Seamus, too.

And I could finally breathe again. I hadn't noticed that I wasn't until then.

The next morning I was up early as usual, when the sky was the color of a dirty nickel and hadn't yet begun to send out those first yellow and pink and orange fingers of light from a sun just coming close enough to the horizon. By the time I had fed the horses and watered them and then returned to build and light the fire, everybody else was still fast and warm in his bedroll.

We had failed to cross the river into Arizona the evening before and camped on the California side of the Colorado. We were still close enough that I could hear it burbling along if I listened hard enough through Patrick's snores. Patrick could be one hell of a noisy sleeper.

I got the fire going and brought out the breakfast stuff, got the coffee perking and threw some bacon in the fry pan and set some biscuits to baking in a covered skillet, and then I got 'round to the unpleasant business of waking my brothers.

Now, they weren't the most forgiving bodies to rouse, but I had, to a man, figured the best way to motivate them—always from the farthest distance I could muster. It was always with a kick to the boot, too, followed by a quick leap to one side.

I kicked Josiah first, knowing that he was the least likely to kick back. Except this time he did. If I hadn't jumped to the right, just in case, he would have clipped me, sure as anything. He sat up quick, his blankets falling away, while he hoarsely boomed out, "What? What is it?"

"Same's always, Josiah," I said. "It's mornin', and I got your breakfast cookin'."

He gave his eyes a rub, then took a suspicious peek up at the sky, which was still starry. "Looks like it did when I went to sleep."

"No kickin'!" came from Seth's bedroll. He'd

pulled the blanket clear up over his head until you couldn't even see his hair sticking out, and his hat was sitting about two feet away, upside down. "I'm up!"

Everybody began to rouse, except for Franklin.

And then I realized that Franklin wasn't there. His hat was, and when I pushed back his blanket, all I found underneath was his saddle.

"Where'd he go?" asked Seth once he'd sat up. He scratched the back of his head. He glanced over his shoulder, toward the horses. "His gray's still here."

Josiah stood up. "Sure is." He started turning round, scanning the dim horizon in all directions.

His snoring ceased, Patrick sat up, rubbing his eyes. "What's for breakfast?"

Seamus growled, "Shut up, Pat. Our brother's gone."

Sleepy-eyed, Patrick squinted at him and said, "Huh?"

Rance and Ed, Seth's friends, sat on their blankets, looking accusingly from brother to brother.

As he got to his knees, Patrick said, "Aw, he's probably taking a leak somewhere. How come you're all such a bunch of mama hens all of a sudden?"

But Josiah didn't pay him any mind. "Everybody up and fan out. Now!"

We all scrambled, Rance and Ed included.

Seth and I, tripping through the rocks, set off toward the river. Rifle swinging at his side, Josiah went the opposite way. Seamus, followed by a grumbling Patrick, went south, and Rance and Ed went north.

I whispered, "You think something happened to Franklin?"

Seth said, "If he went to take a piss, why'd he take the trouble to slide his saddle clear over and tuck it in? And why'd he leave his hat?"

I had no answer.

We found his body about thirty yards downstream. It wasn't much banged up by the water or rocks. There was a stab wound in his back, and on top of that, his throat was slit from ear to ear. The river had done its work, washing away the blood, so the neck wound gaped wide and without disguise.

"Somebody wanted to make real sure he was all the way dead," Seth said through gritted teeth as I helped him pull the body from the water. "Or at least all the way quiet."

"But why?" I asked, my voice cracking.

"Your guess is as good as mine," he said before he stood up straight and hollered, "Found him!"

Other than Josiah's muttered "Sweet Jesus!" we all stood round Franklin's body in horrified silence.

Anyway, I was pretty much horrified. Can't

rightly think of another word for how I felt. Franklin's face was whiter than milk, and the big, slashed-open veins in his throat oozed pinkish water instead of blood. His eyes were open and blankly staring, the poor sonofabitch.

He sure as hell hadn't done this to himself.

"Well, I figure we can rule out suicide," said Seth, echoing my thoughts.

Josiah nodded.

Rance, who didn't look any too steady, said, "I think Ed and me had best be movin' along. You comin', Seth?"

Seth just shook his head, real slow. He stared at the body on the bank. "On your ways, boys."

Patrick said, "Hey! How do we know they didn't do it?"

Josiah leveled a gaze at him. "And why would they, Patrick? What reason would they have to do in ol' Franklin?"

Patrick couldn't think of one, I guess. Or at least he didn't say anything.

Josiah rumbled, "That's what I thought."

Patrick stood there a second longer, then lifted his face. "You was fighting with him just last night. Over Junior there! How do we know you didn't up and kill him in the middle of the night?"

"I didn't," Josiah said, "but now at least you're usin' your thinker."

Now, me, I didn't figure Franklin was much of a loss, but then, I was in a hurry to get to

Tombstone and Miss Ruby Tulayne. Also, Wyatt Earp, to see if he'd come up with anything more on Daddy's killer.

"Could we dice this out on the road, fellers?" I asked. "I'd sorta like to get back to Tombstone."

"Why?" snapped Patrick. "To see your big friend, Wyatt Earp? I thought you already figured out who shot our daddy. It was that Lannigan character. Besides, what can we get up to there? I mean, what with you being big buddies with the law and everything."

I hadn't wanted to "get up to" anything, and I said so. It seemed like my brothers were born owlhoots, but I had no intention of riding that trail with them.

I said, "Fine, go on and do your business. I'm goin' to Tombstone."

I felt a hand on my collar. "Not so fast, little brother," came Josiah's voice. "Somebody killed Franklin, and I don't figure it's a good idea to split up until we figure out who done it."

I took a deep breath. "All right. But it pains me to hear you think I might be the culprit."

His hand moved to tousle my hair. "Don't believe any such thing, Junior. But when we figure out who did it, we might need you to help hold him down."

That didn't make me feel much better, but I muttered, "Okay, I guess."

While Rance and Ed prepared to leave, I fixed

breakfast, and Seth, Seamus, Patrick, and Josiah pulled Franklin's body a little farther from the banks before they built a stone cairn over it. There were already vultures circling in the silvery morning sky.

13

Nobody said a thing while we ate.

I guess I could say everybody was still in shock over Franklin, but for me, I was wondering just which of us had done him in. I hadn't done it, and I figured Seth was likely blameless, too, mostly because to get up he would have had to elbow me in the ribs. Josiah, too, although I figured he didn't do it mainly because I liked him so much. Also, I thought that if Josiah was going to kill somebody, he wouldn't do it by cover of night. He'd just haul off and kill him dead.

Rance and Ed, well, they didn't have any reason to kill one of us. 'Course, that don't stop some fellers from killing, but Rance and Ed didn't seem like that type. Also, they were kind of scrawny compared to Franklin. They would have made a lot of noise dragging him to the river. Also, if they had stabbed him in his bedroll, they would have made a big bloody mess.

Franklin's blankets showed nary a trace of blood.

I figured that whoever had done it had got Franklin to walk down to the riverside and had stabbed him there. That left Seamus and Patrick. Seamus had the background for it, all right. I mean, he'd killed before. But I couldn't really see him pulling it off, being so short and all.

That left my only full brother of the lot, Patrick.

I kept my mouth shut, though. I wasn't about to go tossing accusations around. Not until I had a chance to talk them out with somebody, at least. And I supposed that somebody would have to be either Seth or Josiah.

I had cooked, so it was Patrick's turn to scrub the dishes, but he declined. Josiah ended up doing it. He said he didn't mind, since we had water for a change. We mounted up again, paying scant attention to Rance and Ed, who had taken off earlier and were now just specks on the distant northern horizon. We had spoken less than fifteen words between us since the makeshift burial.

Josiah spoke. "Don't you think we ought to say some words over Franklin's grave?" he said from atop his horse. Patrick was leading Franklin's horse, Toad, behind his Baywing.

"Why?" asked Patrick, and Seth's brow furrowed.

"We ought," I replied, and reined Consternation up toward the riverbank. Seamus fell in behind me, and the rest came along.

Josiah spoke real powerful over Franklin's resting place. By the time he finished, Seamus was openly weeping, and I had scrubbed away a tear or two myself. I don't know about Patrick. His face was hidden from me. But even Seth, who was no kin to any of us and who was hanging around just out of friendship for Josiah (and lack of anywhere else to go, I guess), looked a little wet around the eyes when Josiah said, "Amen."

"That was awful good, Josiah," I said. "Franklin couldn't have been seen to better if we'd had a real preacher."

"Don't mention it, brother," he replied in a tone that said he meant it.

We forded the river and started southeast, toward Tombstone. At least, that's where I was headed. I don't know about the others. Mayhap they were just following me.

A week later, when we'd ridden halfway across the territory, that's just what I figured out they were doing. I reckon they didn't have anyplace else to go.

*   *   *

Another week or so, and we finally rode into Tombstone. I couldn't have been less prepared for all the changes that had been made since I rode out, all those months ago.

For the main thing, all holy hell had broken out after the Earps' trail for that gunfight I witnessed. In my mind it was little more than a skirmish, but the populace had turned it into practically all-out war.

The Clantons and the McLaurys were even more organized than before and counted Johnny Ringo and Curly Bill Brocius among their company. One of the Earp brothers had been murdered, and Morgan Earp had been shot up so bad that he had left Tombstone along with the other two brothers and their wives, and they said he would never be able to use his arm again.

Only Wyatt remained, and along with Doc, he was leading a posse against Ringo and his ilk.

All of this I got from Ruby Tulayne during a long night at the Westerner Hotel.

"I don't know if he had time to come up with anything," she said to my question about Daddy's murder. "Wyatt's been awful busy."

"Sounds like," I muttered, and rolled toward the wall, disheartened.

"There, there," she whispered, and curled her arm around my shoulders. "Forget about that for tonight if you can, Pat. Let Ruby make it better."

Call me weak, but I did.

Come the morning, I found Seth and what was left of my brothers down at the Russ House, having breakfast. I joined them and brought them up to date on the local news, which nobody seemed much interested in. I was surprised, for I'd thought that they'd be as concerned as I was about Daddy's murder and who had pulled it off.

"Why, hello, Pat!" said Miss Nellie Cashman herself, who was passing by with two big platters of fried eggs and sausages. "And don't you look like a pod full of peas!" She scanned the faces at the table and stopped at Seth. "You can't be a Doyle, can you?"

He blushed. Miss Nellie was so nice, she made everybody blush. "No, ma'am, just a friend of the family."

I noticed that, to a man, there wasn't one head with a hat on it in that big old dining room—mine included. Even Patrick was hatless. I wondered if Josiah had snatched it off him or if he'd taken it off himself.

Likely it was Josiah, because Patrick looked kind of put out and mad.

I didn't much care, though. I dug into my steak and eggs—likely paid for by Patrick with poor Franklin's roll—and ate like a spring bear cub on a first kill. Ruby had surely worked up an appetite in me.

I was halfway toward emptying my plate when Ruby herself appeared in the doorway and motioned toward me. When I got to her, she whispered, "Caught you! Wyatt and Doc just rode into town, honey. You can catch 'em if you hurry direct to the sheriff's office."

I looked longingly at my breakfast, which Josiah was already scraping onto his own plate—there was never a better cook than Miss Nellie—and then back to Ruby. "Thanks," I said, settling my hat atop my head. "Let's go."

Wyatt scrunched up his eyebrows. "Who?"

"Spats Lannigan," I said for the second time. "He's from back east. New York City, to be exact. I got it on good authority that he was out to get Daddy." I went into my little song and dance about Five Points and Tammany Hall and all that.

Wyatt didn't say anything for a minute, and then he turned in his swivel chair and shouted, "Doc!" Doc had gone in the back room.

In a second, Doc poked his head out, his cheeks mostly covered with shaving soap, and asked, "What can I do for you, Wyatt?"

Wyatt pointed at me, and I went through the whole thing again while Doc ran a towel over his half-shaved face.

When I finished, Doc scratched his chin stubble, coughed up some blood into a handkerchief, excused himself for it, then said, "I believe I've heard of some of those men. A long time ago, before I came west. If your daddy tangled with Spats Lannigan, Pat, then he was in some kind of Dutch. 'Course, Spats'd have to be what? Fifty-five, sixty by now? They always did say that Spats came at a man like a freight train. Don't 'spose he'd take too kindly to your daddy traipsin' all over hell and gone for so many years, keeping him from doing Old Smoke's business."

Wyatt looked as flabbergasted as I felt, hearing Doc talk about those names like he'd known them all his life, but I said, "Who's Old Smoke?"

"Gang boss. You got a match there, Wyatt?"

Wyatt pulled out his sulphur tips, and Doc lit a skinny black cigar with one of them before he continued.

"His real name was Bill somethin' or other. But they called him Old Smoke because once, when he was beatin' the pea-waddin' out of some fella in a barroom, he got too close to the stove and his pants caught fire. They said you could smell the stench of burnin' flesh and the smoke was near to blinding. But Old Smoke? He just kept on sluggin'."

Doc looked like he thought that was an admirable trait for a man to have in his character, but I felt myself gulp hard. I know I saw Wyatt have much the same reaction as me.

He said, "Like I always told Virgil, you know the nicest people, Doc."

"They're drawn to me," Doc said, admiring his fingernails. "Moths to the flame, I suppose." He looked up and smiled. " 'Course, I'm not exactly sure if Lannigan was workin' for Old Smoke's mob or the Dead Rabbits. Maybe Old Smoke was in league with the Dead Rabbits, but in any case . . ."

Wyatt cocked a brow. "Dead Rabbits?"

Doc shrugged. "I didn't name the lads, Wyatt. This stuff about Old Smoke, I'm only tellin' what was told to me over a card game I had a while back. In fact, just around the time you lost your daddy, Pat. 'Course, I'd heard of them before, just not in such detail."

"Don't sound like those back-east places are so much better than us, out here in what they call the uncivilized wilderness," Wyatt commented as he lit his own cigar.

"Wait a gol-darned minute!" I fairly shouted. "This feller you had a card game with, Doc?" I reached for my back pants pocket, pulled out the book, and shoved it under his nose. "Did he look anything like this?"

Doc squinted and held the cover picture out at arm's length, cocking his head. "Y'know, I do believe it could be him, if you added on an extra twenty years or so and took him out of those dude clothes."

And then his face got all funny and he looked over at me again. "Son," he said, "if Spats Lannigan was the man who killed your daddy, I do believe this is the gent. If I had known, I would have killed him for you where he sat, whilst he was fillin' my ears full of that New York gangland horse hockey."

"Gimme that," growled Wyatt. He dropped his chair back down on all four, leaned forward, and snatched the book from Doc. He stared at it, too.

"I'll be damned," he finally said. "I believe I've seen this feller walkin' around town. Not recent, but maybe five or seven months back. Doc, do you recollect him saying where he was stayin'?"

I felt like we were making progress for a minute there, but then Doc shook his head in a slow no, and my hopes went *splat*.

There'd be no way to find him now. Too much time had passed. He might be in Mexico or Canada or back in New York.

But Wyatt gave me a little hope. He said, "Can I keep this, Patrick?" For a second I thought my brother, Patrick, had walked in the door behind me! Then I came to my senses and said, "Sure. Keep it as long as you want, Wyatt."

He nodded. "Fine. I'll show it around and ask some questions. Where you stayin'? Miss Nellie's Russ House?"

"Yessir."

"All right, then. I'll keep you posted, Pat." He slipped the book into his desk drawer, then relit his cigar, which had gone out. "So, where you been all these months, kid?"

I told him—well, most of it, but not about the lawbreakers in the family or about Franklin getting murdered by one of our own—and finished up by saying, "Miss Nellie says we all look like peas in a pod."

Doc chuckled. "Now, that I'd like to see."

"Come to the Russ House anytime Miss Nellie's cooking," I said, and stood up. "We'll likely be there."

"I'll do that, boy," Doc said.

Wyatt nodded and said, "Nice to have you back in Tombstone, Pat."

"Good to be back," I said, and let myself outside.

I was shaking by the time I took two steps to the street. The murdering sonofabitch had killed my Daddy, then waltzed straight into town to play cards. For all I knew, I might have walked right past him on the street or swept up his cigar ashes at the Oriental. He might have tossed me a tip. And I would have taken it gladly.

Filled with some weird mixture of horror and

consternation and plain black anger, I slowly walked back, through Tombstone's already teeming streets, to the Russ House to try and wrap my brain around it.

14

Seth met me before I got all the way there. He just grabbed my arm and swung me around the opposite way.

I yelped. "Hey!"

He hissed, "I wouldn't go in there right now if I was you, Junior. Patrick's got himself all worked up."

"What is it this time?"

"Oh, Seamus called both him and Josiah niggers." He tried to pull me up the street, but I wasn't budging. Seamus calling Patrick that word was the same as if he'd said it to me. We had the same ma, after all. Maybe that made us both colored, too, but I hated that word, hated it when it was used in conjunction with a colored man, like Josiah, or an Indian.

"That damned Mick!" I said, before I realized that name applied to me, too. I'd been called it enough, growing up.

"Easy there, Junior," Seth said. "Glass houses, y'know." We began moving up the street, through the crowds. "Maybe you could tell me who that shapely young thing was what called you away from your breakfast?"

"An old friend," I said, still trying to straighten out the mess in my mind. "Ruby Tulayne."

He smiled. "She your girlfriend?"

I'd never thought about it before. I suppose you could say she was, but then, I suppose you could say she was half of Tombstone's girlfriend. But then, she'd never charged me so much as a wood nickel, so I said, "I guess so, yeah."

His face fell some. "And that was where you spent the night? At her place?"

I shrugged.

"Well, it's always the quiet ones, like my ma used to say. 'Course, she should have known. My pa, Hall Winters, was a quiet man, too. Had half the gals in the county draggin' on his sleeves and the hems of his britches, but he always came home to Ma."

"Thought you said your ma was dead."

"True. But after that, he always came home to Aunt Alice."

I stopped walking. "Your pa married your dead ma's sister?"

He gave a shrug of his shoulders. "Three of 'em, actually. And then their cousin, Becka. He always said that Simpson women don't last long, but they're the finest kind as long as they hold up. He was just on his honeymoon with Arva when I up and left. He was crazy in love with her. 'Course, he was crazy in love with all of 'em, while they was around.''

I felt the corners of my mouth quirk up, and I shook my head. "Seth Winters, your whole family's daft!"

"Thought I could get a chuckle out of you. You were lookin' pretty grim there for a while."

I nodded. "I was at the sheriff's office."

Seth's face froze. "You didn't tell him about Franklin, did you?"

"Why are you so worried about that all of a sudden?"

"Not me so much, personally. I just don't want to get locked up and questioned for a couple weeks in some mining town, that's all. I mean, do you know how much things cost?"

He turned my head to the nearest shopfront window and a sign that said, EGGS 2 FOR $1."

I said, "Well, if we're all in jail, at least they'll feed us, won't they?"

He laughed at that, then said, "Word to the wise. I wouldn't go telling Patrick—or any of the others—about your visit."

"Why not?"

"Does this Ruby Tulayne of yours have a sister, Junior?" he asked, and commenced walking again.

*   *   *

By the time Seth and I got back to the Russ House, we found no sign of Josiah, but Patrick sat facing the wall in a deserted dining room, and Seamus was at work in the kitchen, doing dishes.

When I questioned him, a testy Seamus said, "Don't ask me. That Miss Nellie is worse than any schoolmarm I ever had!"

Back out in the dining hall sat Patrick, still nose to the wall.

"Patrick, what happened?" I asked.

Silence.

"Maybe Miss Nellie told him he couldn't talk," ventured Seth, a barely concealed smile trying to creep over his face.

Patrick made a low growling sound deep in his throat.

"As a matter of fact," came Miss Nellie's voice from the doorway to the lobby, "I did. You missed quite a stir, Pat."

"Where'd Josiah go, ma'am?"

"To find Seth. I'm guessing he didn't."

Seth shook his head. "No, ma'am, Miss Nellie."

She picked up a stack of linens off the end of the nearest table and began to pass them out, over the tables. Getting ready for the lunch crowd, I supposed.

"Well," she said, "he'll turn up, I reckon. He might be back, so I'd check your room first. Patrick, you may help me ready the tables, now."

He turned around, muttered, "Yes, Miss Nellie," and proceeded to help her with the tablecloths. He wasn't smiling.

Josiah had come back to Miss Nellie's and was in our room, slumped on the edge of his bed. "Finally," Josiah said when we opened the door. He glared at me, like I'd done something wrong. "*Your* brother called us a passel of niggers he didn't care to be seen with."

I plopped down on the bed opposite him. "Seamus is as much your brother as mine."

"Not from this day on," Josiah said. "He's all yours, brother."

"It's a wonder Miss Nellie didn't have him hanging curtains!" Seth whispered.

"And Patrick, too," Josiah went on. "We'd best watch out, or Patrick will slit our throats like he did Franklin's."

It was the first time any of us had spoken of it. Out loud, anyhow.

I leaned toward him. "Josiah, did you see anything that night? Hear something, maybe?"

"I didn't need to," he said, low. "Didn't he empty out Franklin's pockets clean as a whistle? It was like a hunter taking a head for a trophy!"

I guess I sagged some. "Yeah, I thought about that, too, Josiah. 'Cept I keep thinking that Franklin and Patrick were pretty cozy all along. I mean, they got on good enough, didn't they?"

"Don't matter when a man's got a quick temper like Patrick," Seth said right out loud, and Josiah nodded. "He nearly killed Seamus right after you took off, Seth."

I wanted to ask what we were going to do about it, or if we should do anything, but the feeling in the room had gone all saggy and sad and angry, so I didn't say anything.

Neither did anybody else.

I think it's time I made a confession.

I had always been sort of a hothead. It was my daddy's blood, I'm pretty sure, from what I'd seen of my brothers. But knowing Doc and Wyatt had tossed a bucket of water on my coals, and I had convinced myself to take the higher road.

Even all those months with Patrick being so mean to me, even finding out about Spats Lannigan and suspecting the worst, and then with poor Franklin getting his throat slit and all, I had tried to brush off those bad feelings and urges.

But right then, standing in that rented room at the Russ House with my brothers and Seth? If Spats Lannigan had walked in that room that instant, I would have ripped the veins from his neck with my teeth, and the consequences be damned.

I was madder than I had ever been in my whole life. I felt my veins practically boiling with the poison of it, of wanting to kill someone, to see him die beneath the force of my two hands.

So when Seth said, "Sit down before you fall down, Junior," I up and slugged him right in the jaw.

It was stupid, I know, but I reckon he was just the vent for my mad. He went sailing across the room and landed underneath a window with a loud *boom* and a rattle, his chin lolling on his chest.

I guess I didn't realize how strong I was back then.

Neither did Patrick or Josiah or Seamus, because they all sat there with their mouths open. I turned toward Seamus. "Take it back," I demanded.

"Take what back?"

"Take back what you said about us after I left the Russ House this morning. The nigger thing."

He gulped. He was a lot smaller than Seth, and I guess he reckoned I could send him to Christmas with one good punch.

He said, "All right, I take it back." He must have figured from my expression that this wasn't good enough, because he added, "I'm sorry I ever said it, Junior. Really. I won't never say it again."

In the meantime, Josiah—who never had to be afraid of anybody, least of all me—had gone over to Seth. There was a little pot of posies on the bureau, and he was dumping the water on Seth's face. Seth's jaw was starting to turn colors, almost as bright as the flowers that Seth clenched in his other hand.

"Is he all right, Josiah?" I asked.

"Like you care," snarled Patrick, like he was hoping for a fight to break out.

He almost got his wish, but just when I was turning to belt him one, too, Josiah said, "He's coming 'round."

Something inside me went flat, but I still said, "You better watch yourself, mister," to Patrick before I hurried to Seth's side.

Josiah was patting his cheeks. I leaned in close and said, "Wake up, Seth. I'm right sorry. I didn't mean it. Please be all right!"

Seth opened one eye. "Sure as hell felt like you meant it."

"Well, his jaw's not broke," Josiah announced, and, stuffing the flowers back in their empty pot, he stood up.

"Feels like it is," Seth said. He lifted a hand and felt his jaw, grimaced, then tried to stand up. I helped him to his feet.

"Jeez," he said softly as he slouched against the wall. "That's some kind of right hook you've got there, Junior." I looked down at the place he'd been sitting. He'd cracked and splintered the wallboards with the force of his collision.

"Miss Nellie's gonna be mad," I muttered.

Seth followed my gaze. "And I'm gonna have me some extra bruises." He reached round and felt his back. And made a face.

"Sorry."

"Next time, give a feller some warning, will you?" He turned to look at his face in the mirror. "God, I'll be purple for weeks . . ."

"By the looks of this hamlet, you'll fit right in," said Josiah. "By daylight, the citizens all look to be professional boxers, they're so bruised, dented up, and gimpy. Well, half of 'em, anyway."

"Tombstone's a brawling kind of town," I said, although I'd just made that apparent.

"You should know. You lived here with Dad," Patrick said.

"Stop asking for it," I said, although I doubt I had any of "it" left to give.

"Look at Junior," he said, mocking me. "All tough and mean, hitting his friends and ready to have it out." He stood up and cocked his fists. "Huh, Junior? Wanna have a go at me? Wanna try somebody your own size?"

15

I should have done it.

I should have hauled off and punched him in the face. At least it would have made him look a little less like me.

But I didn't. Seth said, "C'mon, Junior, let's get out of here and get us some fresh air."

I think I nodded. I know I went with him. "I don't know why you're even talkin' to me," I mumbled once we got out in the hall. I was too sorry and too mixed up to say it any louder.

He walked me outside, into the sun. "Come to think of it, I don't know why I'm talkin' to you, either, you big gawky Mick." He smiled when he said it, though.

I smiled back. His jaw had swollen up a lot and was red, black, and blue. He did look pretty comical, although I can't say I admired the fact that it was me who'd put the funny on his face. "C'mon, Seth."

I dragged him to the butcher shop and spent half my remaining few cents to buy a raw steak for him to hold on his jaw. And then, since he wouldn't be seen on the street like that, we ducked into Big Jim Harold's Bar, where he ordered us a couple of beers and sat across the table from me, pressing that slab of bloody beef to his face.

When Big Jim brought the beers, he said, "When you're finished fixin' yer face with that beef, I'll throw it on a fire fer y'all. Fer a few cents."

We each gave him a nickel for the beer, and he went away, grumbling under his breath. I sighed. "Well, that cleans me out. If you want that beef cooked, you're on your own for the cookin' and the eatin', both."

All he said was, "Don't be such a buffalo brain, Junior." And then he pressed something into my hand. It was three dollars, in silver.

I started to say, "But—" but he cut in quick.

"Just shut up and take it," he whispered, then motioned to Big Jim. When Jim—who was called Big because he was broad, not tall—came back, he threw him the steak and said, "Light a fire under it. And you got any potatoes or onions or beans to go with it?"

"Reckon I can dig some up."

"Fine," Seth said, and flipped him two bits. "Don't go cookin' it to death, now."

Big Jim nodded. We watched him disappear

into the back room, the steak swinging at his side and scattering little droplets of steer blood.

"Decided I'd rather wear the badge," Seth explained, "and let you have the breakfast."

All this kindness did was to make me feel that much worse. I hung my head and shook it, slow.

"Aw, cheer up, Junior. At least you didn't knock any teeth loose."

"I'm so sorry," I said. I couldn't look at him.

He ignored my apology. "You finish that book yet?"

I knew which one he meant. I said, "Yeah. But I gave it to the marshal."

"You what?"

His tone made me look up again, head cocked like a spaniel.

"I gave it to Wyatt. Wyatt Earp. For the picture of Spats on the cover."

His face filled with pure amazement. "You *know* Wyatt Earp?"

"So what?"

He shook his head and laughed. "You beat everything, you know that? And I 'spose you know Doc Holliday, too?"

"Sure. Why?" I didn't see what he was getting at.

But all he did was laugh like a jackass.

Not too long after I polished off my steak "breakfast"—which was served to me with fried onions and beans—we were about to leave when a hand landed on my shoulder.

That big, gassy meal had mostly taken my mind off violence, but I still turned 'round quick with my fists cocked.

"Hold yourself there, young sir!" said Doc himself, holding his hands up from the elbows. He was grinning, but I noticed his using hand was tipped a little toward the pocket in which I knew he stored his derringer. He had showed it to me one time when he was drunk.

I unclenched my fists. "Sorry, Doc."

"Would that be Doc *Holliday*?" piped up Seth.

Doc dropped his hands, but lifted one side of his coat to reveal the hip gun he wore in his flashy rig. "Why, yes, it would, young man," he said, both his face and his tone as smooth as a mink. That's when he was most dangerous, and I knew enough to back up a couple steps. More like, it was time to hit the floor, but I didn't. I just stepped backward, right into a chair that just happened to fall over, real noisy.

Everybody in the place lurched at the commotion, excepting Doc. He stood his ground, calm as open water on a windless day. He was still staring at Seth, smiling. "And who might it be that's askin'?"

If Seth had noticed the general unease in the room, he gave no sign. He stuck out his hand and said right out, "Howdy, Doc, sir. I read all about you in the books! Pleased to be makin' your acquaintance!"

Doc relaxed some and took Seth's hand into his. They shook. "Don't go believing everything you read, son," Doc said. Then he turned to me. "This isn't one of your 'peas in a pod' brothers, is it?"

I tried to laugh, but it came out more like a strangled chuckle. "No, Doc. This is my friend Seth."

"Seth Winters, sir," Seth added.

"Sometimes a friend will do you better than a brother," Doc muttered, almost to himself. Then he said to me, "Don't go repeatin' that to Wyatt."

"No, sir," I replied, though I didn't have any idea what he was talking about.

Doc slid his hand away from Seth, who was still mindlessly shaking it. Once free, Doc pulled an already bloodstained handkerchief from his pocket and coughed into it. Clearly, he was a lot sicker than he had been when I was last in town.

"Wyatt wants to see you," he said. "I was just headed to the Russ House to round you up when I spied you from the window."

"Thanks," I said. "Has he got something on Spats Lannigan already?"

"That's for him to tell you. And now, if you two gentlemen will excuse me, I have business to do up at the Striped Garter." He gave his head a shake. "Hasn't been the same since our Irish Jenny left town. Do you remember her, Pat?"

"Can't say as I do."

Doc shook his head. "What a pity, what a pity," he mumbled, and left us, coughing into his handkerchief on his way out to the street.

"Who was Irish Jenny?" asked Seth. "And furthermore, how could you ride right next to anybody for months and never once mention that you know Doc Holliday and Wyatt Earp, for true and personal-like? That don't even pass for human, Junior!"

I was beginning to think I'd hit him too hard or maybe not hard enough. "Calm yourself, Seth. You want to go up to Earp's office with me?"

He was on his feet in an instant. "Do I? Are you foolin'?"

I shook my head and headed for the door, Seth dogging my heels like a puppy. I swear, I was halfway embarrassed for him!

By the time we had walked clear up to the law office, he had calmed down, some at least, and was acting halfway human when we entered to find Wyatt standing behind his desk, talking on the telephone.

He motioned us to take a seat, which we did.

Seth whispered in my ear, "Is he talkin' to himself?"

"No, that's a telephone," I replied, incredulous that he'd never seen or heard of one. "They got a lot of 'em back east, I hear," I commenced, as if I myself knew all about this modern convenience. In truth, I'd seen only the one in Wyatt's office, and only for the first time this morning. "They say that someday everybody will have one right in their house."

Wyatt said, "Thank you, John," then hung up the little earpiece on its metal hook. At last, he turned toward us. "Didn't expect to see you so soon, Pat. Who's your friend there?"

We went through the introductions all 'round, and Seth managed to be fairly calm, considering that I knew he was practically wetting his britches at shaking hands with a Genuine American Hero. He'd informed me that's what Wyatt and Doc were on the walk up. I am not fooling.

Anyhow, if I'd had any hopes that the law had managed to catch Spats Lannigan—or even locate him—between breakfast and lunch, I was sadly mistaken. Wyatt, having dug up a copy of the same book, simply wanted to return mine to me.

He handed the tattered copy across his desk. "Thought you might like to have it back. Ruby Tulayne tells me you're a big reader."

"Thanks," I said, sticking it into my back pocket. Hopefully, I asked, "Don't s'pose you've got any news yet? I mean, about Lannigan?"

He poked a thumb over his shoulder at the telephone. "That was John Clearwater on the horn. He's spreadin' the word."

"Who's John Clearwater?" Seth asked. I was glad he did, because I didn't know, either.

"At the U.S. Marshals' office, up to Prescott," Wyatt replied, then stood up. "Now, if you boys'll excuse me, I'm goin' home to get some damn sleep. Doc and I have to hit the trail again before sunset, and I have not slept for forty-eight hours."

"Sure, Wyatt, sure," I said as he walked 'round the desk. I rose, pulling Seth out of his chair at the same time, and we all left together, though we parted once we hit the street.

"Holy cripes, why are you acting like such a dingleberry?" I asked Seth once we got clear of Wyatt's earshot.

Seth's eyes got all round and his brow furrowed, like I was the stupid one. "Are you loco, Junior? Wyatt Earp and Doc Holliday?" He sighed deeply, and added, "Why don't you just tell me the names of all the people you've met in your life, in case there are five or six others that are famous the whole world over that you didn't know about?" And then he pulled down his hat brim and started walking purposefully toward the Russ House.

It took three long strides to catch up with him. "I knew they were famous in Tombstone, but I don't know about the whole world, Seth!"

He rolled those green eyes and said, "Sometimes you beat everythin', Junior. Just everythin'," and he kept walking.

Later on, Josiah, Seth, and I took our lunch together, Patrick apparently having forgiven Seamus, since the both of them had disappeared. And right over Miss Nellie's apple pie with cheddar, Josiah brought up the subject I was hoping we'd never discuss again.

"So, boys, shouldn't we be doing something about getting to the bottom of Franklin's murder?" He slanted a glance at me. "Shouldn't we at least be mentioning it to the law?" He had been listening to Seth go on all about Wyatt for the last half hour, so I guess he figured I had legal connections.

I opened my mouth, but Seth beat me to actually saying it. "Josiah, that happened clear over to the Colorado River. Ain't in nobody's jurisdiction, far as I can figure."

I nodded, but then a thought popped into my head and was immediately turned into speech. "Wyatt's with the U.S. Marshals," I heard myself say, although I couldn't believe it. How could I be so stupid?

I tried to cover quickly with, "But we can't say anything, or Seamus'll go to jail for that killin', and you and me will go to jail for breakin' him out, Josiah!"

A picture came into my mind, of Franklin's

neck all cut open and the way those big severed veins, once bursting with living blood, weakly trickled watery pink.

I gagged on my pie and set the fork down.

"One way or another," Josiah said cryptically after a second.

Seth stopped in the middle of chewing and arched a sandy brow. "Huh?"

Josiah didn't reply.

"Josiah, you ain't thinkin' what I think you are, are you?"

Josiah helped himself to another piece of pie.

"What is it?" I said. "What are you two talkin' about?"

Josiah finally spoke. He turned toward me a little and said, "Never mind, Junior. Sometimes these things just sort of take care of themselves."

Seth snorted, but me, I didn't pursue it.

Truth be told, I was afraid to.

16

We stayed around town for about three weeks. I got my old job back, which was sweeping out the Oriental Saloon, so I soon had a little money again. Both Patrick and Seamus got themselves separate, private rooms at the Russ House, and we hardly saw them, although Seth said Seamus had got himself a position at the OK Corral, mucking out stalls. I guess Patrick still had enough of Franklin's money to live on.

As for me, Josiah and Seth and I got us a smaller, cheaper room at Miss Nellie's and went about our business: me at the Oriental, Josiah at the gaming tables, and Seth up the street, at the saddle maker's shop. It turned out he had a real talent at tooling leather and had worked at it before.

But late one Saturday night, Seamus came to

our room and woke us. I was barely asleep, having just got in from Ruby's and having a beer. I rolled out and went to the door to let him in.

"What the heck do you want?" I demanded while he squirmed his way in, under my arm. He went to Josiah first and gave him a good shake, then darted to the third bed and gave the same to Seth before Josiah had time to take a swing at him. Josiah always did that if you woke him sudden-like.

"Get up!" he whispered, although it was just short of a shout. "We have to go. *Now!*"

Josiah sat up and rubbed his eyes. "Why?"

"Because Patrick just killed a girl, that's why," he said, yanking open the bureau drawers and grabbing our valises and saddlebags from the corner.

"He didn't *mean* to," he turned and said, probably in reaction to our wall of silence. "It was an accident. Will you start packing?"

I said, "If it was an accident, there won't be any trouble, will there?"

Seth, who had risen and was already stuffing his saddlebags full of socks, said, "Don't be foolin' yourself, Junior. There's always trouble when there's a killing."

"And your friend Wyatt is out chasing cowboys," Josiah said in his deep rumble. He was going for his valise. "You and Patrick look so much alike, I wouldn't be surprised if the town hung *you* for it."

Time was short, and there wasn't any more to waste on questions. Almost before I knew it, we had settled the bill with Miss Nellie's night clerk and were out on the street, hurrying toward the livery. According to Seamus, Patrick had already lit out to the west.

We followed him shortly.

We spied Patrick's dust, caught him up, and cantered on. We didn't stop until nearly dawn, and then we walked our mounts another mile or so, which got us to Apache Bluff, a tiny town with four buildings.

We just sat our horses on a ridge, looking at it with the sun slowly rising at our backs. I was for riding on down and finding a bed. Patrick was dead set against it. But Josiah sided with me—he was as tired as I was—and so did Seth.

In the end, we all slowly rode into the town, which was built into the base of a towering reddish bluff, and had three saguaro cacti for pretend trees. In fact, those saguaros were the only vegetation in sight. The townsfolk must have used the area around them like a town square, because they had a couple of benches set out beside them, all painted up nice and crisp and white.

Nothing was open yet, so we tied our horses at the rail in front of the saloon—which served as the hotel and restaurant, too, according to the sign. Then we all sat on the edge of the boardwalk to wait.

Josiah was the first to speak. "Just what happened back there, Patrick, to force us out of soft beds and into the desert?"

Barely loud enough that anybody heard, Patrick said, "An accident. It was an accident."

"What was an accident?" I asked through clenched teeth. I had just lost another night's sleep to Patrick's follies, and I wasn't in the best of moods.

"From the beginning," said Seth. He looked just about as happy as I was.

Patrick hung his head even lower, and his hat fell off. He picked it up and banged it against his knee, swearing softly, and Josiah said, "You can start anytime now, Patrick."

"Nobody's gonna care about a whore gettin' killed, Josiah!" Patrick spat. "I let Seamus get me all riled up about it, and now I've lost a night's sleep."

"Killing anybody is bound to get somebody mad, Patrick," Josiah said, "even if it was only a whore."

"Whores are people, too, y'know," I cut in. "Just what did you do, you bastard?"

"Calling yourself names again, brother?"

"Don't try to be funny, Patrick. What happened? Who was she?"

He looked at the dirt, not at me. "Told you. She was a whore."

"She had a name, didn't she?"

"Ruby."

I sat up straight. "Ruby Tulayne?"

I was vaguely aware of Josiah, to my left, standing up and moving away. Seth stood, too, grabbing Seamus's sleeve and pulling him back as well.

"Something like that," Patrick muttered, still staring down between his boots. "I picked her up outside the Oriental and we went to her place. She wanted the money first, and I said no, I ain't paying for somethin' I ain't got yet, and what did she plan on, duckin' out the back with it? Well, she slapped me! Can you figure that? A whore slapped my face! So I hit her back. 'Cept I guess I don't know my own strength, 'cause her neck went *crack* and she just crumpled up, right there on the floor. Just like that. I felt her neck and then her wrist, but she was dead. I even held a knife blade under her nose, Junior. Nothin'. So I just ran outta there as fast as I could. End of story."

He may have thought it was the end, but as far as I was concerned, it was just the beginning.

I stood up and faced him. "Stand up, Patrick."

At last he tilted his head up to me. "Why?"

"Because I am goin' to beat the living crud out of you, that's why."

He looked surprised. "Why?"

"Because," I said, my eyes burning hot with unspilled tears, "you killed Ruby Tulayne, the best woman that ever lived."

Now, I'd told Josiah and Seth all about Ruby, but I hadn't said a word to Patrick. After all, we weren't that close. So I didn't wonder that he looked puzzled. I was gratified, though, when he slowly rose to his feet and brought up his fists.

I admit it. I hit him first, just as hard as I could.

It knocked him backward, and he tripped over the stoop and sat down hard on the sidewalk. He didn't stay there long, though. He scrambled to his feet and ran at me, screaming high, like an Irish banshee. He fell on me and it was my turn to fall, but I took him with me.

We began pummeling each other, there in the street, rolling over and over, trading blows that sometimes brought blood, sometimes only pain. I don't know how long we rolled and rolled in the dust, but at last someone, somebody new, planted a boot in my side and yelled, "Cut it out, you two hooligans!"

I heard another thud and realized he'd kicked Patrick this time. "I mean it! Break it up!"

When we both stopped and looked up, a middle-aged man, hair shot through with gray, scratched his head and said, "What are you two, twins?"

"Not hardly," Patrick said as he edged away, then got up. He looked happy that somebody had stopped the fight.

I wasn't, though.

Josiah came over and gave me a hand up. "Easy, kid," he muttered. "Later."

I supposed he meant that I could always finish it later, and he didn't look like he was against it any.

I nodded curtly, then pulled myself up to my full height and stood proud.

"Sorry, sir," I said. "I hope we didn't wake you up."

"Wake me? Hell, you woke half the town with your high jinks! Now, why don't you boys move along and murder each other someplace else? I'm old, and I'm not up to hangin' the victor."

It was only then that I realized there was a badge on his chest. I said, "Yessir. I wouldn't want to put you to any trouble."

I noticed that Seamus was already on his horse, and Josiah and Seth were moving in that direction.

"Well, see that you don't," the sheriff said. "Now, move."

"Yessir," said Patrick and fairly ran toward his horse.

"Thank you for the warnin', sir," I said. Then I tipped my hat and joined the others.

We were clear of that little excuse for a town in two minutes, but I was still angry as sin itself. I guess my face gave me away, because Seth rode up next to me and said, "It'll be all right, Junior. Calm down. You go and kill him, you'll be just as rotten as he is."

"I s'pose." I didn't much care, though. He had murdered Ruby, who I'd gotten to think of as "my girl" even though she was turning as many tricks as ever. But what could I do? I couldn't support her. I could barely support myself.

Silently, tears began to roll down my cheeks. I scrubbed at them with my sleeve, picking up blood and dirt with every swipe, but they wouldn't stop.

"Golly, Junior," Seth said softly. "I knew you liked her, but . . . golly."

I couldn't look at him. I just kept crying while Patrick rode tall and straight in the lead, like he was a captain leading a bunch of raw recruits.

I hated him.

We didn't see another town until we rode into Half Moon Crossing, Arizona Territory, which is just east of the banks of the Colorado River.

We hadn't talked hardly at all on the way across the territory, not any of us, save to ask for the salt or the coffee or to say whose watch it was. Even Josiah and Seth were silent, and I was no more communicative. I kept my nose stuck in my books for the most part. I don't know what the others did. I didn't much care.

We took rooms at the Dude Inn, which was a fancy name for a not-so-fancy hotel, and we took them like we had before: Patrick and Seamus each in a single room, and me, Josiah, and Seth in a triple. I don't know what was wrong with those people in Half Moon Crossing. It took a lot of talking before they'd even let Josiah stay there, let alone share a room with us. When we finally got to our room, I overheard Josiah mumble something about word not having reached this far that the War was over.

As I had got used to not talking, I didn't comment on it, although I thought it was pretty funny. I heard Seth chuckle a mite, though.

Once we had got settled in, it was Josiah who officially broke the silence of almost two weeks. He said, "Well, what are we going to do about Patrick?"

Seth arched his brows and said, "Do? What can we do? We ain't the law."

Josiah said, "Well, he's made it impossible for Junior here to ever go back to Tombstone. Somebody's bound to have seen him, and thought it was Junior. And even though Franklin was no good, I think we're all in agreement that it was Patrick who killed him."

Seth and I nodded slowly. I guess they'd all been thinking the same as me since that day.

"You don't have to hang around, Seth," said Josiah. "This is family business."

"You tellin' me to go away?" Seth's tone had an edge of anger to it.

But Josiah shook his woolly head. "No. Just that you don't have to stay around until the end. That's all. We been friends for a long time, Seth. No reason you should have to get in this trouble, too."

Seth let a little air out of his lungs. "Think I'm already fair deep into it, Josiah. I'll stay."

17

Now, I figured that Spats Lannigan would have headed back east after he killed my daddy. True, it had taken him over two decades to do the deed, but I figured that maybe he'd had other business to take care of, too. And then, Daddy moved around a lot.

So on the whole, we were headed in the wrong direction. That's how I figured it anyhow.

On the second day in Half Moon Crossing, I said something to Josiah. He was shaving at the time, and he looked up from his mirror. "You still out for blood for that, Junior?"

"I believe I am, Josiah." In fact, I was certain that I was.

"And you still got it in for Patrick?"

"You know I do." The death of my fair Ruby was still too fresh for me to hold it any other way. And then there was Franklin.

Josiah wiped his razor on his shoulder towel. "You know, Junior, I don't think it was such a good idea for you to come lookin' for us. So far, all it's led to is a string of thefts and murders." He just stood there, looking at me.

"You're right, Josiah," I finally said. "But I couldn't know that when I started. All I wanted to do was find out about my ma."

"Well," said Josiah as he resumed his shaving, "there you are."

I didn't quite know what to make of that, so I excused myself and went out into the lobby. Seamus was sitting there, looking all slouched and dejected.

I walked right past him at first, then thought better of it and stopped by his chair. "What's wrong?" I asked him.

"Don't you know?" he snapped, then his face softened. "Sorry, Junior. Thought you were Patrick for a second there."

I shrugged, just a little. "So, what's wrong with you?"

"It's your damned brother," he said.

"He's your damned brother, too."

"Yeah, but he looks a lot more like you, so he's yours."

I couldn't argue with him there. Patrick was my full brother, more's the pity, and I was stuck with it. "What'd he do to you, anyway?"

"My money's missin'," he said, head propped

in his hands. "I didn't have much. Only nine dollars and some. But the deal is, it was in my room until last night, when Patrick came in to visit, and then it was gone."

Truth be told, I didn't have much sympathy for him. I said, "Well, you're out nine bucks and I'm out a whole lady friend. The lady who taught me to read. The lady who gave me a home after Daddy got killed. I don't think we're all the way clear yet." I turned on my heel and walked outside.

And ran smack into a female with her arms full of packages. She went sprawling, her parcels went flying, and I caught myself on the hitching rail.

She turned her pretty head toward me. She had long red hair, looked about my age, and she was madder than sin. "You again!" she shouted.

I pulled myself off the rail and went down to her, to give her a hand up. "Me *again*? I've never seen you before, Miss!"

She gave out a little huff, but allowed me to aid her to her feet. "Then who was it that pushed me off the sidewalk before?"

"Wasn't me. I just now came out into the day. If he looked a whole lot like me, it was probably my brother Patrick. I apologize to you on his behalf, Miss."

She twisted up her face—it was still pretty, even screwed up like that—and stared at me, real close. "I suppose it might have been," she said. "But I'm not entirely convinced."

I started picking up her packages. There were seven in all. "Where to?" I asked over the top one.

"The Butterfield office," she said, and fell into step with me as I walked along. "Maybe it wasn't you, after all. That other boy just ran away."

I wasn't surprised. I said, "You'd best lead the way, Miss. I'm new in town, and I don't know my way around yet."

"It's Miss Bower. Evangeline Bower," she said.

I had never heard such a pretty name, and I said so.

She laughed. That was pretty, too. She had blue eyes, almost as light as mine, and a spray of freckles across her little nose. She was tall, too, probably five feet nine or so. I liked that, too. She didn't slouch, like the few other tall girls I'd seen, and even added to it with her wide-brimmed sunbonnet. She seemed proud of her height.

And then she moved ahead of me, and all I could see of her was a snatch of her blue dress, through the top two parcels I carried. I followed her like a puppy dog, even though those parcels were getting heavier and heavier. What did she have in there, anyway? Anvils?

We turned a corner and walked into the Butterfield office.

"You can put those down here," Evangeline
said and pointed to the counter.

Glad to lighten my load, I set the boxes down
and took a step back from them.

"More jelly, Miss Evangeline?" asked the
plump man behind the counter.

She smiled at him—a glorious smile, it was—
and said, "Yes, Mr. Martin. For St. Louis and
Minneapolis this time."

"Them St. Louie folks sure love your cactus
jelly," Martin replied jovially and began
weighing each box on a scale behind the
counter, then writing its weight on a little pad.

"So far, anyway," Evangeline replied. "I
surely hope they don't change their minds anytime soon." She still hadn't looked over my way,
but only had eyes for her packages and Mr.
Martin's scale. And I just stood there like a dolt,
transfixed. I had never in my life seen such a
pretty, perfect female.

Images of Ruby Tulayne came into my mind,
unbidden. True, Evangeline was prettier than
even Ruby, but Ruby was dead, killed by my
brother's hand. I had no right to be standing in
the Butterfield office, ogling Evangeline, when
Ruby's death remained unavenged.

So I made myself look away from those russet
curls, those sorrel-lashed blue eyes, that straight,

freckled nose, and I stepped out into the street again. I took a deep breath, but I was trembling inside.

This was all Patrick's fault! He'd killed my half brother, my girl, and knocked Evangeline off the sidewalk without so much as a by-your-leave or an apology. Oh, and he'd taken Seamus's money, too!

If Patrick had been standing there at that moment, I likely would have killed him with my bare hands. But he wasn't. He was probably off looking for someone else to rob or murder.

I tried to shove my hands in my pockets, but I couldn't. I'd grown too much in the last months. The cuffs were about halfway up my boot tops, too. This led me to wonder if I was taller than Patrick now. If I was, that might swing things a little in my favor.

"Young man?"

It was Evangeline's voice, and I turned toward it, despite myself.

She said, "I'm so very sorry to ask, but have you a nickel?"

"A nickel?" I stuck two fingers into the narrow confines of my pocket and began to feel for change. I was lucky, and pulled out a nickel.

As I handed it over, Evangeline said, "Thank you very much. I'm a tad short. The jelly weighed more than I thought it did. Here you go, Mr. Martin." She handed him the nickel and took her receipt from his fingers. Then she joined me on the sidewalk. "If you'll come to my house, I can repay you."

"There's no need—"

"Yes, there certainly is," she stated, and gripping my elbow, started walking back the way she'd come.

I kept pace with her—although I was a little surprised that a girl could walk that fast—and kept telling myself not to think about the way she looked. And the way she sounded. Her voice, there in that dry and dusty town, was like a clear mountain stream, quenching parts of me I didn't know I had.

Before I knew it, we had turned several corners and come to a small adobe house, painted blue and surrounded by a picket fence. She opened the gate, and we went up to the porch. "You'll wait here a moment?" she asked.

"Yes'm," I mumbled, my throat being thick, and I stood there while she went inside.

I heard her talking with another woman—older, and likely her mother—and then she appeared again and pressed a nickel into my hand. "Mother would like to know," she began, "if you'd care to share some limeade with us."

I felt my head nodding yes. "That sounds fine, Miss Evangeline," I said, and followed her inside the house, then out the back door to the patio. There was a little fountain in the center of it, and a table sat on the periphery, in the shade of two lime trees. She sat at the table, and I joined her.

I hunted for something to say and came up with, "So you ship cactus jelly all the way to St. Louis?"

She smiled. "Yes, we do."

"You and your mama?"

She nodded.

"You make it, too?"

"Of course!" She laughed a little.

Her mother appeared from the house carrying three glasses and a pitcher, and joined us. The daughter was the mother's child all right, right down to the freckles. She was smiling, too.

"Thank you for coming to my daughter's aid, young man," she said as she poured.

"It was the least I could do after I knocked her off the sidewalk," I said.

Mrs. Bower stopped pouring and looked up at me, then over at Evangeline. "What?"

Evangeline giggled. "Oh, it was an accident, Mother. Nothing to remark about."

The pouring resumed. "If you say so, dear. And just what is your young gentleman's name?"

Evangeline blushed, and quickly I said, "Patrick Doyle, Junior, Mrs. Bower. At your service. I'm late of Tombstone."

She handed me a glass. "We hear bad things about Tombstone, Mr. Doyle."

"It's a pretty rough town, ma'am, I'll grant you that," I said, and left it at that.

"Well, then," she said, and we all lifted our glasses.

In my whole life, I have never tasted such good limeade.

That night there was a big ruckus at the hotel. They woke us with their banging around and shouting, and if that wasn't enough, two men broke down our door!

All three of us sat up like startled prairie dogs popping out of their holes, and then a third man stepped in and pointed at me.

"That's him," he said in a definite kind of voice.

Before I realized it, they'd dragged me out of bed, pulled me out into the hall, and marched me out of the hotel and to the jail.

When I heard the cell door slam, I finally got my voice back. "What did I do?" I wailed. "What did I do?"

"You know what you did, you murderin' thief," growled one man. He had a badge pinned to his chest.

"Or thievin' killer," said the second man. He locked the cell door, then put the keys in the desk.

"Well, that's that," said the sheriff, as if now everything was all right. And then he and the other man blew out the lantern and left me alone in the dark, half naked in my long johns.

18

Seth came by first thing in the morning, carrying my clothes and saddlebags. The deputy, whose name was Hanks, had a real spree searching my books for guns and knives and other implements of mayhem, but found none. He dumped my precious books through the bars with his skinny hands, like the fact that I could read made him all the more certain that I'd done the crime.

Which, as a matter of fact, I hadn't yet been told about.

Seth asked him but got much the same as me, except Deputy Hanks told him to get the hell out and shut the hell up. Me, he just told to shut the hell up.

The deputy said that a lot—"hell," I mean. He was a real cussing machine.

Anyhow, Seth waited until the sheriff came

on duty to try visiting me again. He pulled out a chair opposite the sheriff's desk, and said, "Sheriff Rufus, just what is my friend, here, charged with? I can't see that he could have done much more than fart in his sleep. Is that a criminal offense in Half Moon Crossing?"

Sheriff Rufus glared at him. "He stabbed a Mexican over on Fourth Street. There were witnesses."

"But I never been on Fourth Street!" I yelped from inside the cell.

"Shut the hell up, you peckerwood," Deputy Hanks said. He was leaning against the filing cabinets while he carefully trimmed his mustache in a little mirror he had propped up against some files. Every once in a while, he'd stop and make faces in the mirror, like he was expecting to find something startling there. And when he didn't, he just went back to snipping again, one hair at a time.

"Shut up, kid." The sheriff himself barked at me. "And don't try to tell me you were never over there. Like I said, I got witnesses. Three of 'em, and they all seen you plain as day."

Seth and I looked at each other and at the same time we both said, "Patrick!"

Seth then set in telling Sheriff Rufus about my grand journey up from Tombstone and the gathering up of the brothers. He didn't say anything about how Franklin stole that poor old trapper's life savings or how we found Franklin with his throat cut there in the Colorado River—I guess he figured I already had enough going against me without adding another unsolved murder to the mix—or about me and Josiah busting Seamus out of jail to prevent his hanging.

But he did say as how we all looked a lot alike, especially me and Patrick, on account of we shared the same ma and pa, and how Patrick was a hothead who had skipped out on the hotel sometime last night and gone who knows where.

"He did?" I asked.

Seth turned toward me. "Seamus went to get him this morning, and his room was empty. All his stuff was gone, and his horse from the livery, too." His expression alone told me how bad he felt.

The sheriff folded his arms and sat back, like all this was news to him. And like he didn't believe a word of it.

Seth twisted back to him. "Go and check if you don't believe me. Check the hotel, check the livery stable. The clerk at the hotel has seen 'em both at the same time!" he added in a rush.

Sheriff Rufus glowered. "You'd best not be makin' this up."

Seth folded his arms, too. "Go ask, and you'll see I ain't lyin'."

Sheriff Rufus didn't even say good-bye. He

just shoved his chair back with a loud scrape and walked out the door, leaving Seth and me and the deputy, who had finished with his mustache. It looked just the same to me.

He set his beady eyes on Seth. "You get the hell out, too, you little bastard."

Seth stood up and turned to me. "See you later, Junior," he said with a little smile and a wink that I figured was supposed to cheer me some. "I'll be waitin' outside."

Once Deputy Hanks went off duty, I finally had a chance to talk to Seth. Josiah came with him this time, and they both pulled up chairs outside my cell. Seamus didn't come.

"Rufus told me he checked everything out, like I told him."

My face hurt, I was all of a sudden smiling so hard. "When do they let me out?"

All of a sudden Seth didn't look so cheerful. He said, "They don't."

"They figure they've got a suspect, and that's you, Junior," Josiah said. He was looking at the floor between his boots.

"But aren't they even gonna look for him? Josiah? Seth? Aren't they even gonna try?"

Josiah slowly shook his head.

"Sheriff said it ain't worth it for a Mex," Seth added. "Too hard to get a posse together. And it don't look like he's gonna try."

Josiah grunted, disgusted-like.

I swear, I would have cried if I was by myself. I just couldn't believe it, couldn't believe the law could be so callous and uncaring, couldn't believe there was no justice in the world.

"But don't worry, Junior," Seth said.

My brow shot up. "Don't worry? Are you crazy?"

"Me and Josiah and Seamus, we're formin' our own posse. We'll track him down." He didn't sound all that sure, but I appreciated the effort.

Weakly, I said, "Thanks, boys."

Josiah looked up and smiled a little. "Sounds like you've got a cat caught in your throat, Junior."

"S'pose I do." It was my turn to stare at the floorboards. "Sure appreciate you bringin' my clothes and books, Seth."

I heard him stand up. Josiah, too. Reluctantly, I lifted my head. "You goin' now?"

"Settin' right out," Seth said. "Seamus is down to the livery, settling our bill and gettin' the horses ready to go."

I stuck my hand through the bars and took Josiah's hand. I shook it. "Thanks. I'm proud to have you for a brother."

He grinned. "You can let go anytime, Junior."

Embarrassed, I did. But Seth grabbed my hand and shook it enthusiastically. "We'll find him, Junior. Don't fret too much."

"Thanks, Seth. Thanks for everything." I

wanted to add, *That's including your friendship, too*, my heart was too full.

I sat in that lousy jail for three whole weeks, waiting for some word from Seth and my brothers, waiting for the circuit judge to arrive, and waiting for Deputy Hanks to drop dead. He was so full of horse hockey—and spread it around at every opportunity—that by the end of week one I could have throttled him with my bare hands. Then, at least, they'd have real reason to hang me.

As for Sheriff Rufus, he hardly spoke a word to me. Maybe he felt bad because he knew he was going to hang the wrong man, but then again, maybe he was just plain hard and didn't care. I finally decided on the last one. Any man who wouldn't make an effort to find the true criminal wasn't worth my spit, so far as I was concerned.

I guessed he didn't figure I was worth his spit, either.

One by one, they marched the witnesses in to identify me, and each and every one said that I was the killer. I heard one of them say that Patrick was walking down the street talking out loud to himself when the Mexican man—whose name I gathered was Miguel Cordoba—accidentally bumped into him. And Patrick flew into a rage out of all proportion to the incident. He pulled a knife from his boot, and the rest, like they say, was history.

You know, looking back on it now, I figure that my brother Patrick would have been maybe diagnosed as a schizophrenic if they'd known about such things in those days. Nowadays they know better and they would have taken measures, but they still don't do much but lock them away someplace, the same as somebody should have done with Patrick years before.

I remembered Mama saying as how he was odd, but I can't believe she really didn't know just how odd he was. And I remembered her telling about her mother, how she got so crazy at the end. Truth be told, I spent a few sleepless nights wondering if it was in me, too.

But it wasn't in Mama—the craziness, I mean—and she'd said it started early with Patrick, when he tried to burn down his boarding school and all when he was just a kid. Or maybe it started even earlier than that. Maybe that's why she tried to send him away in the first place.

But it was too late to second-guess anybody now. I just hoped my brothers and Seth were having some luck tracking Patrick down. You know, it wasn't like I wanted to see him hang. Of course, I didn't want to hang in his place, either. I just hoped that they'd judge him criminally insane and put him away. That was better than hanging any day of the week, so far as I was concerned.

Of course, I don't know that Patrick would have agreed with me.

The judge came at last, and still no word from my brothers.

They tried me in the saloon, that being the biggest building in town. I guess they expected a crowd, and they sure got one. They set up rows and rows of chairs, and they were all filled. I kept looking for Evangeline, but she didn't show up. I figured she was probably embarrassed to admit she knew me.

I couldn't say I blamed her, but it would have been nice to see a friendly face.

All through the trial—well, the time I got to be on the stand, anyhow—I proclaimed my innocence and told them about Patrick, and how my brothers had gone looking to bring him back.

It didn't do much good. Even my own lawyer didn't believe me, and the sheriff didn't care one way or the other.

Needless to say, the verdict came in "guilty as charged," and I was sentenced to hang by the neck until I was dead on the following Saturday noon. It was way too soon to suit me, and I said so. Several times.

The sheriff just hauled me back to jail and locked me up.

"Won't you send somebody to look for my brothers and Seth, at least?" I pleaded with him.

He poured himself a cup of coffee. "Just where you think we ought to look?"

"I—I don't know."

"And that's why I ain't doin' it."

And then I had a sterling idea. I don't know why I hadn't thought of it earlier. I said, "You can send for our ma, up in Mourning Dove. They used to call it Greased Weasel. It's in the San Francisco Peaks. She'll tell you the truth about Patrick, and about me!"

He'd sat at his desk while I was talking, and now he set his coffee mug down. "Son, I couldn't get a man up there let alone back inside a week, even if he could find the place, and a week is what you got left." He picked up his coffee mug and took a sip. "If it makes any difference, I'm right sorry. Sometimes things just work out bad for a man."

Well I was real surprised to hear him say that, but I had a tough time believing him. He hadn't acted sorry at all. I said, "And sometimes things work out bad even for a sheriff. My brothers and my friend Seth will be back with Patrick, you'll see."

He only grunted.

19

The next day, they started to build the gallows, which they constructed right outside my window. I couldn't help but look at it. I thought this was extra cruel, but who would listen to me? Deputy Hanks just kept telling me to shut the hell up, and Sheriff Rufus ignored me entirely.

But on the Tuesday before I was to hang, I had a visitor. Evangeline. I was so happy to see her I nearly burst, but I felt bad that she had to see the inside of a jail, even for a few moments.

"Pat," she said, "I'm so sorry." She looked like she meant it, too, especially when she reached through the bars and took my hand in hers.

"I'm awful glad to see you, too, Miss Evangeline, but you'd best not stay long. Somebody will see, and your reputation'll be ruined."

She smiled, but it was a sad one. "I'm sorry I didn't come sooner. When Mother heard about what you did, she forbade me."

"But I didn't do it, Evangeline! It was my brother Patrick. He's sick or crazy or something!"

"Ouch!" she exclaimed. "You're holding my hand too hard!"

I let go. I had got too upset, telling her about Patrick. "Sorry," I said. "Sorry."

Sheriff Rufus looked up from the seed catalog he'd had his nose stuck in. "Miss Evangeline, you know this brother of his?"

She replied, "I should say so! He nearly pushed me in front of a freight wagon!"

Rufus's brow knitted, like maybe he was finally interested in this thing. "You see 'em together?"

"No, but I can tell them apart after a little staring. The main difference, however, is that Pat is a fine young man, while his brother is a churlish cad."

I felt myself flush.

"Also, he could not have changed his clothes or his demeanor in the time between him pushing me into the street and my meeting Pat here."

Rufus opened his catalog again. "Won't hold up in court, Miss Evangeline. First off, you still didn't see them together. Second, it's only a female's testimony. And weak at that. Just forget about this mess and go back to puttin' up your preserves."

Evangeline shot right up out of her chair.

"Sheriff Rufus! Shame on you!" she scolded. For a minute there, I thought that red hair of hers would burst into flame.

But all Rufus said was, "That's the truth of the matter. Can't change it."

"What's the truth? That I'm an addlepated woman who can't tell the difference between two men?"

Rufus put down his reading matter once again. "The truth is that Miguel Cordoba was one of our leading citizens, even if he was Mexican. He owned the bank, for God's sake! And every man in this town wants to see somebody hang for his murder, 'specially now that the bank's been inherited by his brother, Julio, and Julio ain't near so kindhearted as his brother was. Somebody's got to pay for this, Miss Evangeline, and that somebody is your friend in the cell."

"But it wasn't him!" she said, near tears. "I know it wasn't him." She began to sob.

"Don't worry, Evangeline," I said, although there was little force behind it. "My other brothers have gone looking for him. They'll be back any day now."

"Better hurry," said Sheriff Rufus flatly. He was back to studying his catalog, and didn't look up at either of us.

*   *   *

Evangeline dropped by later in the day to bring me some books. I thought that was awfully nice of her, considering her mother thought I was a killer. She brought a couple of real novels, not the dime kind, a couple of half-dimers, and a schoolbook. It was geography. Until I got that book, I never knew just how far away New York City was from Arizona. I traced my journey on a map inside, too. We had sure traveled a long route, my brothers and I.

The two real books she brought turned out to be both writ by some English lady. They were *Pride and Prejudice* and another I don't remember the name of. I didn't get very far in either of them, since they were set in the olden times, over in England.

The real treasure turned out to be one of the half-dimers, because it was a new release and because it mentioned Spats Lannigan. According to the writer, Lannigan, after "taking care of some old business in Arizona," had returned to California, where he now made his home. Or at least, where he did most of his murderous tramping around.

I underlined the passage, dog-eared the page, and wrote on the cover, "Josiah, read page 76."

I knew that "old business" Lannigan had taken care of in Arizona was shooting my daddy.

Friday came, and still nothing from my brothers or Seth. They were going to hang me tomorrow, and I had given up hope of ever seeing them again, let alone getting my vengeance on Spats Lannigan. Deputy Hanks was purposely mean to me, chanting, "Gonna hang your sorry ass till you're dead, dead, dead," over and over again.

At least the sheriff told him to shut up whenever he came in the office, which wasn't very often these days. I think he was having second thoughts, but I can't be sure.

And then it was Saturday morning. I was supposed to die at noon, and I can't say I didn't about stare that clock to death, too. The crowd started to gather around the scaffold at about eleven thirty. They were excited about my imminent murder-by-committee, and there was some shouting and catcalling.

I can't say I was too happy about the crowd—let alone anything else—even though they brought me a good meal of a big steak, fried potatoes, and slab of chocolate cake, frosted pretty.

I couldn't finish it, though. Mostly because I lingered too long over it, and Deputy Hanks dragged me from my cell.

He cuffed me behind my back so I wouldn't try anything "funny," and then he made me stand in the middle of the room. In a few minutes, the sheriff walked in, accompanied by a preacher with a Bible in his hand.

Deputy Hanks drew his gun and nudged me in the back with its barrel. We all walked out into the sunshine, although I only noticed it was sunny because it hurt my eyes. We walked toward the scaffold while the preacher read from the Good Book. I thought his choices of passages were strange—he was mostly reading from Revelation—but I didn't say anything, mostly because Deputy Hanks had threatened to gag me if I made any trouble.

I figured hanging would be bad enough without a gag in my mouth, too.

I was just mounting the steps when, over the crowd, I heard somebody shout, "Stop! Stop it, you fools!"

It was Seth! He was alone, though, and my heart, which seemed to have risen in my chest, dropped down to my feet.

He jumped off his horse and pushed his way through the crowd until he faced the sheriff. "You can't hang him now!" he said, yelling over the hum and buzz of the throng.

The sheriff looked at him and said, "Yes, I can. And I'm gonna. Now, get your butt out of the way."

But Seth stood his ground. He said, "We found Patrick, Junior."

My heart began to rise again. "W-where?"

"He went home, to your mama's place. Sheriff, Josiah and Seamus are comin' right behind me. They've got him. And he confessed on the trail. We all heard him."

I'm not exactly sure what happened next, as I passed out, right there on the gallows steps. When I woke up I was behind bars again—and for the first time, darn glad to be there. Seth was still there, and Josiah and Seamus were wrestling Patrick through the office door.

"Well, I'll be corn-holed and left for dead," exclaimed Deputy Hanks. "There *is* two of 'em!" His face was a sight, it was twitching so fast.

"Looks like it," remarked Sheriff Rufus.

"We gotta have a trial all over again?" asked Hanks.

"All over again," said Rufus.

Hanks lit up like it was Christmas. I guess he liked trials. I know he figured to have a new whipping boy to torment, and on top of that, one who looked like me.

He walked over to the cell, unlocked it, and yanked the door open. He pointed at me. "You, get your ass the hell outta there." I stood up and started gathering my things.

He twitched his finger between Josiah and Seamus. "And you two, throw the new one in."

Me and Patrick traded places, and the first thing I did when I walked out of that cell was to drop all my books and throw my arms around Josiah, Seth, and Seamus. I don't remember which one was first, but later all three claimed I had about squeezed them to death. They didn't much mind, though.

We had to stay in town for Patrick's trial. In the end, he confessed right out in public, and I was legally cleared of the crime. After my testimony, they voted to send him to the Arizona Prison for the Criminally Insane, with a life sentence. I was glad they didn't hang him, but Josiah thought otherwise.

"How come they were gonna hang you, but they're just sending him off to the loony bin?" he asked over and over. "It isn't fair, Junior."

"How many times I got to tell you?" Seth said. "Ain't nothin' fair about life."

"I've heard that before," I muttered.

Josiah said, "Oh, shut your pieholes, the both of you," and went back to putting his things together. We'd be leaving soon. It didn't seem soon enough to suit Josiah, though.

But there was something I had to do. Seth knew what it was, and he winked at me when I exited the room. I took off down the street and walked all the way to Evangeline's house.

Her mama answered the door and just stood there staring before she asked, "Are you the one they're sending to the loony bin or the other one?"

"It's me, ma'am, Junior Doyle. If I came at a

bad time, well . . ." I started to back up, toward the steps.

"Wait," she said, and at last opened the door and ushered me inside. "I'm sorry, son," she added, fiddling with a dishcloth. "It's just you two look so much alike . . ."

"I know, ma'am. Don't feel bad. I'm sorry."

And then she started to cry!

I stopped right where I stood, and she stopped, too, and then I took her hands as gentle as I could, and said, "Please don't cry, Mrs. Bower, or you'll get me going, too!"

She all of a sudden lifted her arms and threw them around me and began to full-out sob. And so did I. I couldn't help it!

I heard a screen door slam, looked toward the sound, and there came Evangeline, her head shaking. "Now you break this up, you two," she said, her voice light and playful, and her red hair glistening in the sun coming from behind her. "Mama, now, really! Let him go, would you?"

With Evangeline's help, her ma managed to pull away at last, and Evangeline escorted her to another room in the house while I got myself pulled back together. I tell you, emotional women get to me every time.

Finally, when I had myself put back together, Evangeline came back up the hall. She stopped and took my hand, then she led me out to the backyard.

Softly, I asked, "Is your mama all right?"

She led me to a chair at the table, and I sat down. She sat across from me.

"Yes, she'll be fine, sooner or later." There was a hint of a smile lurking at the corners of her mouth.

I wasn't any too certain about that smile of hers. My eyebrows took turns going up and down, over and over again.

"Don't worry, Pat," she said. "And stop that. Your eyebrows will fall off." The hint of a smile on her mouth widened, and my brows ceased their dance.

I said, "Yes'm, Miss Evangeline."

And then she laughed, and everything was all right again. She seemed disappointed when I told her we were leaving today, though, and asked why I had to go with them.

"It's the man who shot our daddy," I explained. "He's over in California."

She looked down at her lap. "Shot him right in front of you, didn't he?"

"Yes'm."

"After you . . . finish with him, will you come back through?" She looked up again, and right at me.

"For certain," I said, and across the table I gripped her hands in mine. Hers were so tiny, but so warm. I really wanted to latch on to more of her, but I'm a man of manners.

So instead, I let go of her and stood up and said, "I'll be back, Miss Evangeline."

"Yes, Pat," she said with a sad smile. "I know you will. Would you . . . would you like me to wait for you? Official-like?"

I had been afraid to even broach the subject, but now that she had, it was all right. Everything was all right! I said, "Boy howdy, Miss Evangeline! Would you?"

20

Evangeline had kissed me so hard and long that I could still feel the soft burn of her full and rosy lips as I walked back to the hotel, and I had a grin on my face that seemed permanently affixed.

In fact, when I finally got up to the hotel, Josiah was stepping out the door, and he stopped just long enough to smack me across the face.

I was holding my hand to my swollen cheek when Seth, then Seamus came out. "Better go pay your bill off," said Seamus, seeming secretly tickled, and he followed the others down the street, toward the livery.

I believe I was whistling when I walked in and set into grooming Consternation. I had kept up with grooming him every morning when I was able and had paid the hostler extra to brush him the mornings I couldn't, but he'd been out rolling in the corral and he was plenty dirty. I can tell you, I raised some dust that morning!

Seth, who was grooming his Sand Bar just outside Consternation's stall, made some noise. And when I looked over, he had an expression on his face that made me stop my whistling. I guess he didn't want Josiah to hear it, because he nodded that way, then back at me. Well, I stopped whistling, but I couldn't stop myself from humming the same happy little tune.

I didn't even notice the stall door swinging open and Josiah coming up until he was right beside me and stopped my brushing hand with his arm. "Knock it off," he growled, low and dead serious.

"You may think this is all sunlight and roses," he said, once I'd stopped and looked over at him, "but we been through this whole thing before. For you. I don't see much difference, between manhunts, so shut the hell up."

I just stood in Consternation's stall, frozen to the spot, until he left and went back up the aisle to his own horse, Hooker. Seamus was already mounted up on Kilkenny and sat there in the middle of the barn, waiting for the rest of us.

I joined them last, and we all four rode out of the barn: following his lead, following him west, following him back toward the border and California.

I guess it was because we were brothers that they all knew I wanted to see Spats Lannigan dead. Maybe they wanted it as bad as I did. In any case, it was as if we had all signed a document, legal and binding, to trail him to the end.

It was funny, because if you'd asked me six months ago what I wanted with Spats Lannigan, I would have said, "Nothing." He had killed my daddy, but I had decided to let bygones be bygones. But it seemed that, somewhere along the line, I had reversed my position on that topic. I wanted to see this Lannigan for myself, wanted to see him bleed.

I wanted to see him die.

I was going to avenge my daddy, by God, and nothing was going to stop me—least of all my brothers, who were practically leading me to him. I guessed that they wanted some revenge, too, and just figured to let me take care of it for them.

It was all the same to me.

When we reached the river and the ferry, Seamus paid all our fares. Midriver, when I went to thank him, he said, "Don't. I know what you're goin' to do, and tossin' out money is the least I can do to help it along. I ain't good for anythin' more than that, so don't go thankin' me. I figure it's the least you got comin'."

I grabbed hold of the side rail and asked, "Why, Seamus? Don't you wanna see him dead as much as anybody?"

He said, "Sure. But you're the one who got

us all together, and you're the one we all been followin'. We're just taggin' along to cover your ass, boy."

It was kind of odd to have somebody look up at you—from a whole foot lower—and call you "boy," but he did.

But that didn't hit me right at the moment. I just knew I was mad. "My butt doesn't need covering, Seamus! I can do just fine on my own. I don't need you boys to tag along and toss in a lightning bolt if I should happen to need a spare!"

He stared at me for a moment before he said, "Fine enough, then. You're on your own as far as I'm concerned, boy. I'm off to go up and meet with Doreen and let her know about Patrick and Franklin. She deserves to know, don't she? And Junior, the best o' luck to those who remain with you."

I just stared at him, wondering why in the world he'd want to go off to meet our sister when there was Daddy's death to be avenged. It was Josiah who put a stop to it. His big, dark palm came between me and Seamus, and he turned me away from Seamus and toward him.

"Don't get your knickers in a knot, Junior," he said, which only made me madder. And then he had the nerve to laugh.

Now, in the beginning, Josiah had been the

tallest of any of us, but I seemed to have gained an edge—maybe a couple of inches. He was still intimidating, but not so much as he had been six months ago. I pushed him away without a second thought.

Crack!

When his fist hit my chin, my whole body flew backward and I landed with my back against Hooker's shoulder and then slid into a squat against the opposite rail of the boat. Hooker was spooked, but she wasn't as afraid of me as I was that she'd land a hoof in one of my soft spots—and that included most of me!

Josiah stepped in, though, and as mad as he was at me, he calmed his mare first before he reached down and grabbed me by my throat. With one smooth motion, he dragged me up off the rail and stood me up in the center of that boat. I guess I just stood there, shaking.

Well, I think anybody would have! Especially when they've just been hit by their favorite brother, and for no reason!

"Josiah! You hit me!" I shouted in a half whine, one hand to my wounded chin.

"You want me to do it again?" he roared, and closed the narrow gap between us.

I cowered a little. Well, I cowered a lot. "No!" I whispered.

He jutted his head toward mine—although at the moment, he had to stick it down, not up—and growled, "Then shut the fuck up, Junior. You're not gonna have to face Lannigan by yourself, y'know. You got me and Seth for certain sure, no matter who takes off." I glanced over his shoulder just long enough to see Seamus with his back turned, doing his best to avoid us entirely.

I said, "You don't have to talk bad to get my attention, Josiah. I know you and Seth are true."

He pulled his big head back to sit square on his shoulders and looked at me. Not that he'd stopped looking at me the whole time. I stared straight back—mostly to hide my shaking hands, which I had clasped behind me—and tried to think of something else to say.

But Josiah didn't give me a chance. He just turned and walked off, as quick and smart as you please, which left me blinking and wondering just what the heck had happened.

"Aw, don't mind him," said Seth, at my elbow, and I jumped about a foot, landing against Josiah's mount again. This time, though, I didn't slide down to the bottom of the boat. I grabbed hold of her mane and patted her, calming her as much as myself with my whispered, "Easy, now, easy."

Seth grabbed my arm and said, "Are you all

right, Junior? Don't let Josiah scare you none. He's on your side."

"Could've fooled me," I managed, in a half-way normal tone.

"Well, he is, and so am I. Just don't go frettin' about nothing. Okay?"

In truth, I was still jelly on the inside, but I looked him square in the eye and said, "Don't worry about it none, Seth. I know I don't need to worry about you runnin' off."

Seamus turned toward me then, quick as a wink, and glared. "It's my business where I go and what I do. It's always been my business and nobody else's. Don't see any reason to go changing that now."

"I didn't argue with you, did I?" I said. I had let go of Josiah's mare by then and stepped clear, lest she begin to act like her owner and just savage me.

I had completely lost track of Josiah by then, but I think I should be forgiven that oversight. My attention was riveted on Seamus.

And I should say for brother Seamus that he didn't cower, as I had when Josiah approached me. He was real brave for a man only five feet eight inches tall, that Seamus. "No," he finally allowed. "You didn't."

From the back end of the boat came Josiah's bass rumble. "You both remember that." And then he walked forward, toward us. It was all

I could do not to duck, just on instinct, but when he came up alongside me, all he said was, "Get your horse ready. We're comin' in to dock."

We were indeed.

I checked Consternation's saddle riggings and untied him while Seamus did the same with Kilkenny, Josiah with Hooker, and Seth with Sand Bar. We all led our mounts to the center of the boat just as she docked and the ferryman dropped the plank. I led Consternation, which he seemed to favor, while Josiah swung a leg over Hooker and just rode her off. The other two followed us on foot, leading their mounts.

While Seamus hopped up on Kilkenny the second all four of his hooves were on dry land, Seth led Sand Bar a good fifty feet from the river, alongside me and Consternation. I mounted just before he did, and I heard him whisper, "You got nothing but dry land now, old son, so don't embarrass me and go to buckin' like a hoppy-toad."

I put a hand across my mouth to hide my smile. It stung, because it landed where my brother's fist had. In fact, my chin throbbed for most of that day. I just ignored it, though. There wasn't much else I could do, riding alongside Josiah and Seth, and for the first half of the day, Seamus.

Seamus left us at about midday. While we

continued northeast, he went due north. He didn't say good-bye—not to any of us—but I watched him disappear into the distance with something akin to sadness. He was already a killer and would probably get himself into worse trouble, but he was my brother.

And he was the third one I'd lost.

21

Josiah, I learned, had been all over the place. Mostly this was on account of his mama, who tended to move in big hops instead of little ones. Once, she moved all the way from Kansas to Texas, and then she moved again, from Texas to Oregon! Those were the biggest ones, though, and with three kids in tow. 'Course, she usually moved when she had a man, and according to Josiah, this was fairly often. Both the moves and the men.

Lately, though, she had stopped doing it, because she had died a few years back. Josiah had turned civil toward me the second we got off the ferry, back down south. I still didn't understand why he had got so riled at me, and frankly, I was afraid to ask him. Every time I mentioned the thought of it to Seth, he shook his head no, like it would be a big sin or something, and shushed me.

I finally decided I'd never learn what I'd done to make him so mad at me back on the ferry, and I just shut up about it. It still bothered me, though. But seeing as he was the only brother I had close enough to talk to, I let it go. He seemed to have let go of it, too. At least, he never mentioned it.

We never saw Seamus again. Not ever. I heard some years later than he'd been hanged in Wyoming for horse stealing, but it was the sort of thing I expected. I can't say it affected me much when I got wind of it. I was sad, sure, but my heart wasn't broken or anything.

But I'm getting way ahead of myself.

We rode north and west, slowly working our way over to the coast, which was a big thing for Seth. He had never seen the ocean before, and we took the afternoon off to give him time to revel in the waves. He sure did, too. I don't think I have ever seen somebody enjoy a natural thing the way that Seth had fun in the waves that day.

I had to warn him not to swim out too far, lest he get in trouble. I had swum out too far one time and almost got eaten by a shark. If Daddy hadn't been nearby in a boat and fished me out, I would have gone the way that his friend, Jesus Mondragon, did. And that way was in pieces.

All Daddy and Bill Stryker, who was along that day, ever found of Jesus was most of his head except for the right ear and part of his nose, and his left foot, up to just past the ankle. We buried them right there, on the shore, and Daddy and Bill said not to ever say how Jesus had died to his widow.

Or anybody else, for that matter.

I didn't ever speak of it, either.

If I was a woman, I'd sure hate to find out that my husband had died like a minnow on the line, only without a line.

We stopped in town after town, following Spats Lannigan's trail. He wasn't exactly trying to avoid us, so it was pretty easy. The hard part was catching up with him. By the time we got up to Sacramento, though, I began to see some hope.

We rode into town nice and peaceable and followed Josiah to a ratty-looking hotel set on a back street. He got down off his horse, handed me the reins, and said, "Hold her for me, Junior." I glanced over at Seth, but he sat his horse, waiting, too.

Josiah went in the hotel for about five minutes, then came out again, shaking his head. "Not this one," he said as he retrieved his horse and remounted. "Let's keep trying."

Altogether, we went and inquired at five hotels—all of the same "look" as the first— before Josiah came out with a smile on his big face. "He was here last night," he announced, after he'd mounted up again. "Stayed in room twelve, and lit out this morning before dawn. Went up north, according to the clerk." He pursed his lips.

"What?" Seth asked.

"I think we oughta ask at the livery, too," said Josiah quietly.

There was one just up the street, but Josiah didn't stop. He said the clerk told him that "Mr. Lannigan" had put his horse up at Kellogg's, around the corner, so we went there. It was arranged so that Spats could have probably looked out his window and seen his horse. He did that on purpose, I supposed. After all, he was a wanted man. By us, at least, and probably a lot of other people, too.

Josiah tossed me his reins again and walked off, into the livery. Seth and I watched while he had a lively conversation with the man there.

"What's he askin'?" I said.

Seth shrugged. "What he needs to, I guess." He was no help at all, that Seth, and I was getting kind of mad.

I was just about to get off my horse when Josiah came back out again and took Hooker's reins from me. And then he stopped and stared at me. "Well, go ahead," he said.

"Go ahead and what?" I asked, kind of surly.

Josiah rolled his eyes. "Get down off your horse. You too, Seth. We're gonna leave the nags for a good feed, and go have us one, too."

He didn't have to ask me twice to hop off

Consternation, but I still doubted him. "Where we gonna eat?" I asked. "I ain't got no—"

"Don't worry about it, Junior." Josiah grabbed my reins and Seth's and led all three horses into the livery, where he handed them over to the stableman. "C'mon," he said, once he rejoined us. "He told me a good place to eat."

"They got steak?" Seth asked as we started walking down the street. It was downtown, but there were lots of houses, too.

"Yeah, they got steak."

"Did you ask him?"

"Seth, don't you know by now, I always ask?"

"Reckon I do," Seth said after some thought.

I hadn't said anything so far. I was wondering how I was going to pay for my dinner with the paltry three pennies I had in my pocket. Well, mayhap I could just have a piece of bread.

Josiah turned so quick that I almost ran into him, but caught myself in time and found we were inside a scuffed room, filled with scuffed tables and chairs and weary, scuffed-looking people.

"Here's a table," Josiah announced, and herded us toward a front window. Well, *the* front window. They only had the one. We three sat at a table for four, and Josiah put his hat on the empty chair. "Don't mind the cost," he said as he got himself comfortable. "It's all on me, fellers."

While we wolfed down our good luncheon of steak, mashed potatoes and gravy, cole slaw, new peas with butter, warm biscuits with honey, and a dessert of baked apples with plenty of whipped cream, Josiah got to business and asked us when we wanted to catch up with the killer Spats Lannigan.

He looked right at me when he asked it, too.

"I don't know," I said, spoon poised before my mouth. I was already to my dessert by then, and boy, it was good! "Does it matter when we catch him, so long as we do?"

"It matters because if he gets to San Francisco and rabbits into a hole, it might be months before he pokes his head out again."

I lowered my spoon and frowned. "Then before San Francisco. I don't want to make this my life's work."

I was thinking about Evangeline, waiting for me back in Half Moon Crossing. 'Course, I hadn't got so far that I'd thought what to do with her once I got her. Marry her, of course, but what then? I had no trade, no way to support her. We couldn't live off her jelly money for the rest of our lives.

Well, mayhap we could, but I wasn't up to thinking that far ahead at that moment.

Josiah said, "Good, Junior. That was what I was gonna recommend. Can I suggest that we sleep for a few hours at the stable, and get out of town while it's still dark? I think we've got a good chance of tracking tonight. Moon's full, and the man at the stable told me he re-shod Lannigan's horse with a bar, left front."

Seth nodded, and chewing, said, "Easy to track."

"Right," said Josiah. He stabbed his last three peas up so they wouldn't go to waste, and popped them in his mouth. He looked at me again. "All right, Junior?"

I nodded, and finally took that bite of my apple and whipped cream. My eyes must have gone round with the pure pleasure of it, because both Josiah and Seth laughed and grabbed up their dessert plates quick to guard them, and dug straight in.

We slept the afternoon away in a rear stall at the livery, and made ready to ride out at about four thirty. Josiah insisted that we stop by the restaurant again and buy a beef sandwich each, wrapped in brown paper, for eating while we rode.

We left town like that, gnawing on the good sandwiches in our hands and heading north while we stared at the ground, watching for

Lannigan's hoofprints. I found a left hoofprint with a barred shoe, but unfortunately it had been made by a horse who'd been harnessed with three others and pulling a wagon. It was a good five miles beyond the edge of town before he turned off it, and another mile before we were able to sort out Lannigan's tracks from the others.

His horse's new shoe turned out to have a recessed bar, which the stableman hadn't mentioned, and which was only apparent when the ground was soft and loamy.

I was glad that the stableman wasn't with us at that moment, because Josiah was awful mad, growling and grumbling under his breath and smacking his thigh with his reins.

But at last Seth solved our problem when he announced that Lannigan's horse toed in a little at the right rear. This was easier to follow than an invisible bar in front, and Josiah stopped grumbling.

There was enough moon that we followed him until almost three in the morning, when clouds moved in to cover the moon. We made a scant camp, slept, and rose at five to be off again. We did not bother to fix breakfast, as Josiah had got us each an extra beef sandwich that he had secreted in his saddlebags.

Nothing tastes better than cold roast beef

when you're riding on a cold, dark California morning, I can tell you that for sure.

I was beginning to get my belly tied up some, though. It was just from knowing that Lannigan was close, that we were getting closer to Daddy's killer all the time. It not only tied my stomach in knots, it jiggled those knots back and forth, so that I felt like I had a belly full of angry badgers.

It might have been the breakfast meat was going bad, though. I knew that about an hour after we finished breakfast, Seth had to dismount in a hurry and squat behind a bush for an awful long time. And then, not fifteen minutes later, he whoaed us and did it again.

The tracks left the little dirt road and went back into the trees, and of course, we followed. Lannigan had done us a favor, for it was far easier to pick his tracks out from those of the deer and such than it was to keep them straight on the open roadway. It was light then, too, and Josiah, riding in the lead, spurred us into a jog so as to move faster.

I hoped that Seth wouldn't have to stop and be sick again, or Josiah would probably leave him behind.

I didn't have to worry long, though. Within fifteen minutes of entering the wood, Josiah held up his hand and we all stopped. I rode up next to him and reined in, my gaze following his pointing finger.

In an old beaver meadow, what was left of a tiny fire still smoked. Next to it was tied a palomino horse, who grazed placidly, and on the other side of the fire was a man. He had just awakened, and was sitting up and stretching his arms.

"Well?" asked Josiah. "Go ahead and shoot. There he is."

I gulped audibly. I kept staring at the man down by the fire, but I heard Seth ride up on the other side of Josiah.

"Are you sure?" I whispered. "I mean, what if it isn't him?"

"It's him." Josiah sounded firm. "That's the horse the man at the stable said he was riding. His tracks are the only ones besides deer and rabbit and porcupine we've come across."

"There was some javelina, too," Seth offered.

Josiah grunted.

I pulled out my rifle, but I couldn't bring it up to my shoulder. I knew I could hit him from here. I knew if I pretended he was a cactus, I could bull's-eye his very heart and kill him with one shot.

But I couldn't. I just couldn't.

"You want me to do it for you?" Josiah asked, a little testy.

I shook my head. If I was going to get revenge

for my daddy, I reckoned I should be the one. But I also reckoned to be darn sure he was the right one. I whispered, "You wait here, you two," and started Consternation out of the trees and down the hill, toward the little camp.

22

It probably took me all of five minutes to let Consternation walk down that grassy hill toward the little camp, but I swear, it felt like five hours. All kinds of things came rushing into my head, like Daddy showing me a nugget of gold he'd brought out of the earth, and Daddy again, moving around in the tent somewhere or other before he settled in for the night, Ruby Tulayne counting her money and it rattling back into its coffee can, a dam I'd made across a creek somewhere when I was six or seven and Daddy coming and kicking it down, and a million other things. All while my gelding made his way slowly down toward Spats Lannigan's camp.

He had spotted me once I was clear of the trees and he stood there, staring as I picked my way toward him. I reminded myself to smile, and called out, "Howdy!"

He didn't move, but his horse lifted its head at the sound.

In fact, he didn't move a muscle until I was fifteen feet away from him and stopped my horse. I said, "Would you be the fella they call Lannigan?"

Still, nothing. Just his stare, which I imagined to be taking on a dangerous quality.

"The man at the stable, back in Sacramento? He told me about that flashy palomino you're ridin'."

"So?"

I was trying like hell to bring up that rifle that dangled from my fingers, but I just couldn't do it. I said, "What's he called by?"

"Horse," he said, real curt. "What're you after, boyo? I'm a man with scant time to waste palavering with day-trippers."

That he had called me a day-tripper made me mad until I realized I'd only ever heard my daddy use that word. And then I got madder.

"Are you the man they call Lannigan?" I asked again, this time more clipped.

In answer, his hand twitched. I was green and young, but I knew what to do. I swung that rifle's business end in his direction, jammed the butt end against my thigh, and pulled the trigger.

My slug took him mid-chest, just as he cleared leather and sent a wild shot into the grass about fifteen feet to my right. It spooked his horse, and even Consternation made a little hop underneath me, but he was dead when he hit the ground.

To make sure, I got down off Consternation and walked over to the body. He was dead, all right. I knelt down and started going through his pockets. He had everything in there. Money, of course, plus Wanted posters—all of himself—a railroad pass, two brass advertising tokens, a copy of a dime novel called *Boss Brennan and Big Navajo Uprising* (which I took, of course), a couple spare collar pins, a tin of chewing tobacco, and on and on.

"You'd best take that money," Josiah said from right beside me, and I jumped. He put a hand on my shoulder and said, "Take it easy, Junior. It's all over now."

"Easy for you to say," I muttered.

"Matter of fact, it is," he responded as he stood up. He sounded like he was smiling. I was glad that somebody was happy about this.

"Slick move, Junior," Seth said from the other side. "I never seen nothin' like it!"

"I didn't plan it," I said. I didn't want to take any credit for something I didn't have set up in my mind. Actually, the only thing I had set up in my mind was that I'd ride down there and he'd shoot me as dead as I'd shot him. I knew better than to admit it, though.

But Seth wasn't paying any attention to my

tone of voice, because he said, "Man, that sure was slick! Slicker than snot!"

"Seth," said Josiah, "get your shovel and cover this man's fire."

I heard the sound of his boots scrambling up and away.

Josiah continued, "What you wanna do with him, Junior?"

I looked up from the body. "Bury him?" I honestly didn't know. I hadn't thought that far ahead yet.

"Well, we can do that. But I reckon the right thing to do is take him back to Sacramento and turn him in for the reward. He's worth money, you know."

I opened my mouth, but no sound came out.

"Two thousand," Josiah said, like two thousand was no big deal. Now, I knew he was down to his last couple of bucks, so that couldn't be true.

"Dollars?" I finally managed to get out.

"Yippee!" shouted Seth, and threw his folding shovel in the air.

Josiah said, "Don't get worked up, Seth. It's Junior's." And when Seth opened his mouth to say something, Josiah cut him off with, "Is that your bullet in Lannigan? I don't recollect you drawin' your gun."

Seth's face fell.

Quick, I said, "We'll split it. I never would have found him without you two helpin' me."

Josiah shot me a dirty look, but Seth let out another yell, then went to look for his shovel, skipping all the way through the tall grass.

Soft, Josiah said, "I know you're feeling bad about shooting him, Junior, but don't think sharing the money's going to share the blame for it, too. There shouldn't be any shame in takin' care of the man who killed your pa. Our pa. Probably he killed a lot of other folks' fathers, too. You can take some comfort in that. That he won't be around to do it again."

Slowly, I nodded. "You make sense, Josiah. Thanks. But you'll excuse me if it don't sink all the way in all at once."

He patted me on the shoulder, then walked over, caught the palomino, and began to saddle him up.

On the way back into Sacramento, Josiah had Seth ride Lannigan's palomino mare and strapped Lannigan across Seth's sorrel. He said he figured that if folks knew Lannigan rode a palomino, it might throw them off a hair. I saw the wisdom in it, even if Seth made faces behind Josiah's back for the first mile or two, or at least until he figured out the palomino was a nicer ride than he'd had on his sorrel, even if he had to stop every few minutes to go squat behind a bush.

I had to laugh at him, and then he got annoyed at me for being so tickled.

You know, sometimes you just couldn't win with Seth.

Anyhow, we rode all the way back to town, asked directions to the sheriff's office, found it, and turned in the body. The whole process was easier than I'd imagined it'd be. The sheriff just asked my name and age and where I was from, and what had happened. And I told him. I also told him that Lannigan had shot my daddy.

He hadn't known that. He pulled out a pad and pencil and wrote down the details, and then he went to the small safe behind the desk and dialed the combination. Before I knew what had hit me, me and Josiah and Seth were standing on the street and there was three thousand dollars in my hand. The reward had gone up since the last poster Josiah had seen. This was fine with me, because three thousand was a lot easier to cut into three pieces than two thousand. At least it came out nice and even.

So there we were, thousandaires, foot loose in Sacramento. We went back to the hotel Lannigan had stayed at and checked in, although there was some trouble until I told the clerk that we'd all be staying in the same room. He didn't want Josiah to have a single for some reason I still to this day can't figure out. I mean, it wasn't even a nice hotel, and the Civil War had been over for a lot of years.

Anyway, we got ourselves a room—finally—and me and Josiah went to get something to eat.

Seth still didn't feel like eating anything, but we promised to bring him back something anyway, in case he changed his mind. He still didn't look too good, though, although he'd stopped having to run for cover and squat every few seconds.

He said he'd got all emptied out, he thought. I didn't doubt him. He even looked skinnier.

Josiah turned out to be even more hungry than Seth looked. He ordered himself a twenty-four-ounce steak, complete with trimmings, and then ordered a sixteen-ouncer when he'd cleaned the first plates. He even finished it, and had apple pie for dessert!

For my part, I made my way through a sixteen-ounce steak with corn on the cob on the side and a green salad, and joined him in the pie. We ordered the same as I'd had for Seth, just in case, and had it wrapped to carry out. They charged a dime extra for the plates, which they promised to give back if we brought them back.

On the way back to the hotel, Josiah asked me, "Well, what now, kid?"

"What you mean, what now?"

"What are you going to do now, that's what now," he replied, shifting the bags with Seth's dinner in them. "I mean, you got Lannigan. That's why you rounded us all up, wasn't it?"

I stopped, and he stopped, too, and faced me. "Well, wasn't it?"

I shook my head. "No, it wasn't! I wanted to

see y'all, to lay my eyeballs on you, that was all! Honest, Josiah, I wasn't lookin' for somebody to help me kill him. Or to kill him for me, either."

He stood there thinking, then kind of cocked his head to one side. "Then you're not gonna disappear in the night?"

"Of course not!"

"Seth would feel right bad if you did that."

I was getting sort of mad. "Josiah, I'm not gonna stand here and listen to you accuse me of stuff I never thought about. You're bein' silly and pigheaded and downright . . . well, and downright *somethin'*!"

He held up one hand, palm out. "Settle down, Junior. Sorry if I jumped to the wrong conclusion." He chuckled softly, which only made me madder.

"Stop laughin' at me, Josiah!"

He clapped me on the shoulder. "Laughin' *with* you, Junior, just laughin' with you. And at me. C'mon, let's get back to the hotel and make sure Seth ain't gone and shat himself to death."

I grinned back, and we went on down the street, to the hotel and Seth.

23

That night, I lay in my bed staring at the ceiling long after the others were asleep. Well, Seth had been asleep when we came in, and flat-out nothing would rouse him. Josiah said he'd be all right, though, and I trusted him.

I was thinking about all I'd been through in what I had just realized was the past year. It didn't seem possible that a whole year had passed since I'd last seen Daddy. It didn't seem a year since I'd laid him underground. But it was, almost exact by the calendar. There in the dark, I let my tears flow silently.

I mourned not only Daddy, but Franklin and Patrick and the absence of little Seamus, who I was certain would come to a bad end without someone to watch over him. And I mourned Ruby Tulayne, too, God bless her. She had been a good woman with a good heart. I vowed to buy her a nice headstone once I got back to Tombstone.

But then I all of a sudden remembered my sweet Evangeline Bower—soon to be Evangeline Doyle—waiting back down in Half Moon Crossing. My tears dried, and a smile stretched across my face.

Evangeline. I'd thought she was the only one who was keeping me going, giving me something to live for, but now I realized there was Josiah and Seth, too. I had taken them for granted. But they were the ones who had stuck by me, weren't they?

They'd seen it through to the end: Patrick's letting me take the blame for killing that Mexican back in Half Moon Crossing, then digging Patrick out from under his rock up in Mourning Dove and the subsequent soothing that Mama must have needed . . . I thought, too, about Seamus calling me and Josiah and Patrick niggers because our skin wasn't pure Irish white like his, and how Seamus had thought he was better than all of us.

Well, like Daddy had always been fond of saying, you just have to wait to the end to see what shakes out and what stays put.

Josiah and Seamus hadn't shaken out, that was for certain.

Now I had to decide what I was going to do next. Besides marry Evangeline, that was.

I didn't decide on anything until I went to sleep, and when I woke in the morning, I couldn't remember what I'd decided.

When I woke up, Josiah was already up and gone, and Seth was eating his cold steak with his bare hands. He looked at me and grinned. "Finally!" he crowed. He must have been feeling some better.

"What time is it?" I asked. "Where's Josiah at?"

"Almost noon, and he went to get our nags." He took another big bite, one that I was sure would keep him silent for a good five minutes.

But it didn't. "Best get dressed," he said around a mouthful of meat. "We got to check out shortly."

I noticed that although he was eating in bed, atop his covers, he was already dressed from boots to hat. I got myself the same way, which didn't take much work—I had slept in most of my clothes. I found the thunder jar and made my morning water, and was just buttoning up when Josiah came in.

"All right, boys," he said, all grand and glorious, "the horses are outside and the rooms are settled up. Let's move it!"

Around a mouthful of cold steak, Seth said, "Aw, can't you bring the damn horse up to me just one time?"

Josiah picked him up by the scruff of his neck and dragged him off the bed. "I ain't your body servant, boy."

"I was only sayin'—" Seth started, but didn't finish because Josiah had pushed him out into the hall by then, with his saddlebags in one hand and his steak in the other. "Crimenitlies!" Seth groused as I followed them out into the hallway, my possessions in tow. "You're sure touchy in the mornin', Josiah."

"Not touchy," said Josiah, leading us down the stairs. "Just enthusiastic. Can't wait to see what Junior has cooked up for us next!"

I stopped in my tracks, held on to the railing, and hung my head. "I don't have the slightest idea, Josiah."

They were down at the bottom of the stairs, looking up at me. And Seth was still gnawing on what was left of his steak.

Josiah gave his shoulders a shrug, then said, "You'll think of something. Over breakfast. Wasn't there some girl back in Half Moon Crossing?"

I fairly ran them over to get to the horses.

After a hearty breakfast—paid for entirely by Spats Lannigan's reward money—we headed back to Half Moon Crossing and she who waited for me there. I know that sounds sort of highfalutin, but that's how I began to think of her—"she who waits for me." I couldn't help but put her in poetical terms.

Josiah and Seth seemed more than content to just ride along, and I was past fine with that. I was overjoyed, in fact. They were more than a brother and a friend, more than hangers-on. They had become as much a part of me as my right leg, and just as important. I never imagined getting married without them there.

We had traveled nearly to the Colorado River before I had the presence of mind to ask Josiah about Faye, Patrick's and my mother. That was thoughtless, I know. She should have been the first thing on my mind, all along. But Josiah told me that she knew, when they rode off with Patrick, what was going to happen. She cried, he said, but she told Patrick to go along in no uncertain terms.

"I think she thought they were gonna hang him," he said as we rode along. "I think she started mournin' him the minute we told her what was happening to you down here."

I couldn't do anything but stare at Consternation's neck. I wanted to get back to Half Moon Crossing and Evangeline in the worst possible hurry, but my brain finally took hold of my heart. "We should go up to Mourning Dove first," I said, and reined Consternation down to a dead stop.

But Seth said, "No, you should go to Half

Moon Crossing first. Josiah and me talked about it. We figured you should get married first, then go up to see your ma."

"He's right," said Josiah, nodding seriously.

I said, "You talked about this? Without me?"

Josiah said, "You're my little brother." And that was that, I guess, because he nudged his horse ahead, toward the river, and Seth went with him.

I followed them, shaking my head.

When we rode into Half Moon Crossing, I was still kind of confused. Josiah said that Ma had a pair of handcuffs hid behind her stove, which was the only way they managed to get Patrick out of there. Josiah said, too, that he'd nearly strangled Seth in the process.

Seth told Josiah to mind his own beeswax.

And that was all the more of the story I got from them, period.

I guess we weren't what you'd call a "talky" family.

Anyway, we checked back into the same hotel, left our horses at the same place we'd kept them before, and I walked up to Evangeline's house.

I was kind of a mess. I don't mean messy-looking, for I had got cleaned up at the hotel. But my brain was tying itself up in knots. I kept thinking about Patrick, and then I'd slip over into Evangeline and where would we live and what would I do, and then it'd go back to Patrick again, and if my dear mama would ever want to see my face again.

I tell you, it was like battling a full-fledged juggernaut. I hadn't come close to a firm grip on anything when I knocked at Evangeline's door.

Her ma answered, and I nearly keeled over at the surprise of it. But then, I wasn't thinking very straight at the time. I think I asked if Miss Evangeline was home, because her ma asked me in the house, then took me to the sitting room and left me there to wait.

In a small matter of time, I heard Evangeline's dainty steps coming up the hall, and I clambered to my feet again automatically just before she turned the corner to join me.

She stopped stock-still, a frozen smile on her lips.

But it was melting.

I think I stammered a bit, but I finally managed to get out, "Evangeline?"

Her lips moved, but nothing emerged. And then at last she said, "Paddy? Y-you're b-back?" She sounded like she had just run the fifty-yard dash.

I dropped my hat and went to her, scooping her shoulders into my hands and pulling her to me, saying, "Evangeline! What's wrong?"

She hiccuped through her tears a few times

before she managed to blurt out, "You came back!"

At least, that's what I thought she said, since her voice was muffled by my vest.

"Of course, Evangeline! Of course I came back." I lifted her chin to see her face. I wanted to know if it was happy or sad.

It was beaming, even though she was crying, and I was suddenly so joyous that I picked her up and twirled her around about three times! She started laughing then, and I kissed her. I don't just mean I kissed her—I mean I kissed her like the whole world was going to end inside one minute and I had to give her everything I had and transfer every feeling I felt in that one kiss.

It must have been a good one for her, too, because she just flat passed out. I'm serious. For a second, I thought I had killed her, and I shouted her name.

But then her eyelashes fluttered a little, and I kissed her forehead, and she woke. Smiling up at me.

I don't think I've ever been so relieved in my whole life.

I helped her to her feet and the first thing out of my mouth was, "Where's the nearest preacher?"

She didn't believe in fooling around, either. We got wed that very afternoon before a justice of the peace, with Seth and Josiah and Evangeline's mama for our witnesses. I gave Evangeline a gold ring that I bought there in town, at the jeweler's. It fit her perfect.

Her mama didn't raise one objection, which I thought kind of odd. In fact, she seemed glad to see her only daughter married off, even though I was practically a stranger to her. We all had dinner together, after the ceremony, and I tried to tell her a little about myself, but found there wasn't much to tell. Anyway, not much you'd tell a lady, much less the mother of the woman you'd just married.

"Just enjoy yourself," Seth whispered into my ear. "She ain't listenin' anyhow."

She wasn't, either. Josiah was entertaining her with stories about the gold camps up in California, most of which I'd never heard before. Pretty soon me and Evangeline were roped in, too, and hanging on every syllable.

Well, we were already wed, and nobody could change that, ever. So I had a new constant in my life. Before, all I'd had that I thought would never go away was Daddy.

So much for that.

But now, I had a brother and a friend and a wife and a mother-in-law. And I knew that unless God chose to take one of them from me, I'd have them my whole life. It was an awful comforting thought. I mean, God'd had His fingers in my business a lot this past year. He ought to be satisfied for a good long time.

After dinner, we parted company, and Evangeline and I went back to the hotel, to the fancy bridal suite I'd rented for the night. Well, actually, I'd rented it kind of on an open-ended basis. For all I knew, we might want to stay there a long time. And I had the money to pay for it.

I carried her across the threshold like Josiah had told me to, locked the door behind us, and the rest was between me and God and Evangeline, not necessarily in that order.

But me and Evangeline were both grinning for at least ten days.

24

Josiah and Seth had threatened to caterwaul and make a lot of noise outside our window, but I guess Evangeline's mama had talked them out of it, because we didn't hear a peep that night.

We sure heard a peep the next morning, although they had the good sense to wait until about ten to come 'round. Josiah and Seth took us to breakfast, and neither of them asked any embarrassing questions just to be funny. I was awful relieved, as I was afraid they'd hurt Evangeline's feelings or maybe make her mad. But they did neither. It was a nice breakfast, too, with flapjacks and hash browns and eggs fixed sunny-side up and fried ham. One thing I found out was that Evangeline liked to eat about as good as I did. I liked that!

In fact, after we left the café and started walking back to the hotel, Evangeline said—right in front of Josiah and Seth—how much she liked my brother and my friend.

I just about busted my buttons, I was so happy and proud.

After about a week of this, Josiah pulled me aside after a big lunch—for which he had paid—and asked me if I had any plans to settle, or were we going to stay in the bridal suite for the rest of our lives?

His question took me aback, 'cause I hadn't even thought about it for the longest while. I guess I was too happy to think ahead much, but he got me to thinking, that's for sure. I said I'd talk it over with Evangeline and get back to him.

He clapped me on the back. "Attaboy, Junior."

"Josiah?" He had started to walk away, but at the mention of his name he turned back toward me and hiked a brow.

I said, "What do you think about ranching?"

"Ranching?" He pushed his hat back. "What the heck are you talkin' about?"

I shook my head. If wishes were horses, beggars would ride—that's what my daddy would have said. "Never mind, Josiah. We'll talk tomorrow, okay?"

"Right."

I went on back up to the hotel, and up to our

room to find Evangeline in front of the mirror, brushing her hair. She smiled at me, and I kissed the back of her neck, then sat down on the edge of the bed.

She swiveled toward me. "What is it, Paddy?"

"I was wonderin'," I said, staring at my knees. "What should we do now?"

"Besides being happy forever and ever?" she asked. She had come over while I wasn't looking, and she settled beside me on the edge of the mattress.

I looked over at her and smiled. "Yeah, besides that."

"What do you want to do, Paddy?" She took my hand. "I mean, what had you planned on doing before I came along?"

I shrugged. "Hadn't got that far, I guess."

She just sat there, both of us quiet as a tomb for a few long minutes, until she said, "Paddy, the whole of the world is open to us. We can do anything we can dream. I didn't mean to tell you right off, but I've got some money saved. Almost three hundred dollars, all from my jelly. That's enough money for us to go anywhere, do anything."

My arm slid around her shoulders, and I pulled her close and kissed the top of her head. "And I've got about nine hundred and some."

She jerked, and then she said, "You've got *what*?"

I smiled down at her. "I plumb forgot. I do, though. Almost a thousand. And I don't know. What do you want to do?"

"But how? Where?"

"I told you, honey. We tracked down my daddy's killer."

"But . . ." She looked confused.

"We tracked him down and killed him." She wasn't looking at me, but I looked away anyhow. "I shot him. I'm not proud of it. But I did, and we split the reward three ways."

I felt her shrink beneath my arm. "Oh, Paddy," she whispered. And then I felt her grow bigger again, like she had taken a big breath and it had inflated her, like a balloon. "Paddy," she whispered in a cracked little voice, "you don't want to be a gunman, do you?"

"No, no!" I said, turning toward her and lifting her chin with my hand. "No, not at all!"

She must have seen the horror on my face, because she pulled me down to her and kissed me, kissed me hard on the lips.

She kissed me so hard, in fact, that my eyes flew open and my man parts went right into business alert. I think she knew, especially since when she broke it off I couldn't form a sentence. I tried, but all that came out was, "H-h-huh?"

She smiled at me. "Then tell me, Patrick Doyle, Junior, what first? Do we want to stay in Arizona?"

I couldn't talk yet. I just nodded. I couldn't think of anywhere else in the whole world I wanted to be except exactly where I was sitting.

And Evangeline smiled at me.

That evening, we had dinner with Seth and Josiah again. Evangeline had got to like them, and they her, for which I was very glad. Wyatt had told me once that it's a bad thing when your wife doesn't like your friends or family. I think maybe he was speaking from personal experience.

That afternoon, before we met for dinner, I had told Evangeline how happy I was that Josiah and Seth seemed to like me so much. She asked if that might have something to do with the thousand dollars I had given each of them, but I said no, I truly didn't think it had a thing to do with that.

Looking back from the considerable distance of all the years since, she must have thought I was daft. I have to hand it to her, though. She didn't even blink, didn't do anything. She just smiled and said, "I believe you, Paddy."

That was all.

And at dinner, she gave me the grandest idea anybody has ever had. It made me the man I am today, and I daresay it made Josiah and Seth, as well.

Evangeline took a drink of her water, there at

Aunt Tot's Café, and said right out, "Why don't you fellows go into business together? I mean, you all get along real good, don't you? You could buy a ranch, maybe."

And that was it. We ended up buying a big chunk of land—2,400 acres—down around Tucson. We ranched some cattle, but mostly what we raised were horses—good working cattle ponies. And Evangeline had a few acres of the cactus she liked for her jelly. We turned a nice profit on the horses and the jelly, too. In time, we switched to registered quarter horses, then Appaloosas, then back to quarter horses again.

The jelly was always the same, though. Except for the name. Evangeline changed it to Double D Bar W Ranch Jelly after a while. She liked the sound of it. Me and Seth and Josiah did, too.

After a while, I paid back the cash money that was owed to Mr. Boudreaux, plus fifty dollars for his trouble. We dug up our sister, too, although when we found her, we had to lose her fast. A more troublesome, quarrelsome woman I have yet to come across!

Even when Arizona got statehood and I got elected to the U.S. Senate, we still kept the ranch. Seth and Josiah were there to work it, you know? And I got myself officially off the hook with the Tombstone authorities long before that. Before we even started shopping for the ranch, me and the others made a side trip down to Tombstone to have a visit with the authorities.

The Earps and Doc were all gone by then, but Sheriff Rufus from up in Half Moon Crossing wrote a detailed letter to the Tombstone officials that made everything clear, and then I was officially off the hook. And that was it. I didn't tell Evangeline or anybody else, but I did buy a tombstone for Ruby Tulayne while we were down there. It was a real nice one, made of pink granite and shipped down from Phoenix, special.

I figured it was the least poor Ruby deserved. After all, the last thing she had seen on this earth was Patrick's face. My face. I still feel terrible about that.

Patrick did all right, too, I guess. He escaped three times, but they always caught him. He died young, at forty-seven, there in the state sanitarium, mostly from self-inflicted wounds. He wouldn't stop banging his head on the bars those last few years.

We did well, those years on the ranch. We started out in one house, then two, then three when Josiah took a wife. Old Seth, he didn't get married until clear into the twenties. He was in his sixties and his bride was a forty-year-old widow from Tucson. No man ever had such a good or thoughtful wife as Seth, except for me.

Josiah didn't fare so well. He married a colored woman, half Indian like me, named Eula. She was real pretty and seemed a perfect fit for the first couple of years, but she got to going to town more and more often. Then one day, she just didn't come back. Josiah rode off to find her and came back, alone, two weeks later. It was another week before he said a word to any of us.

I have never repeated what he told me to another living soul, and neither has Seth, so far as I know.

Epilogue

So here it is, 1950 and halfway through a whole new century.

Old Josiah died in '43, and Seth's due to go any day now. He's up in Phoenix in the hospital, hasn't been able to talk to anybody for almost a year. The doctors up there say he had a bad stroke. I say they've got him hooked up to so many machines that he probably wishes it had been fatal.

Me, too.

I lost my Evangeline just this year. She was fine right up until the end, never even had a cold since the War ended. And I mean World War I. One Sunday evening we were eating our dinner, which I had picked up at the diner in town, when she just stopped talking. Just right in the middle of a sentence. She already had a bite of potato salad forked up and ready to go.

I waited for her to pick up the thought, since we were both kind of getting more addlepated— that's what she used to call it—the last few years. But when I said something, and then something louder with still no response, I got a real bad feeling. She was dead, God bless her. The sentence never got finished, and that forkful of potato salad never got eaten.

We were blessed with two boys, Edgar and Frank. Edgar followed me into public service, although since he'd set himself up in New Mexico, he was a senator from there instead of here. He was—and is—a dad-blasted Republican, too. I suppose there is no second-guessing some people, even when they're your own kids.

Frank (named after my murdered brother Franklin) stayed home in Arizona and taught at the university up in Phoenix until he retired. He was a professor of anthropology. Frank and Lena—that's his wife—gave us two granddaughters and a grandson. Edgar and his wife, Mercedes—the ones over in New Mexico—gave us a granddaughter. Evangeline and I figured we were lucky to get anything at all out of Mercedes.

All the grandkids are grown up and moved away, too. Edgar's girl, Angelina, went to California to try and be an actress. I get a card from her each Christmas, and that's it. She made a few movies you might recognize her from, and she got engaged about every other year, but she never married.

Frank's boy, Wendell, went up to Montana and is just cowboying around, even though he's more than forty now. His older sister—I forgot to tell you, her name is Sherry—married a man from Michigan about seven or eight years back and moved to Detroit. She used to come down here every summer to the ranch, back when she was single. She was quite the horsewoman. Still is, I imagine. She's given us three great-grandkids so far, all of them cute little girls. Wendell's younger sister, Rose (the prettiest little strawberry blonde you ever laid an eye to), never wed, God bless her. She converted and took vows in the Catholic Church.

Evangeline and I had quite a few years together. Almost seventy. I think that must be a record of some kind. I'm well over ninety, which is pretty danged old, even for a former U.S. senator. And especially for a fellow who started out being dragged from one mining camp to another.

Oh, I forgot to say—Mama came to live with us around the turn of the century. She was good to have around, too, not like in those mother-in-law jokes. Evangeline always said Mama Faye was a great comfort to her, since her own mother had run off to somewhere back east with a drummer about four weeks after we got married. Anyway, we never heard much from her—Evangeline's mama, that is—but Faye was always a real pleasure to have around.

She passed on the year before we got our first car. I always thought that was a shame. She would have liked that car, would have liked going fast with the wind in her long, long hair.

That was more than twenty-five or thirty years ago, if I've got things straight. Seems to me she was about as old as I am now. Maybe a touch older.

So that's all, I guess. Just the ramblings of an old man, talking about the old days, when he was a boy and the country was young, and he was wrong about so many things.

We never did see Seamus again, nor ever heard a word. Evangeline always teased me about my brother Seamus, saying he was bound to turn up on the doorstep during those years I was in Washington. She was certain that he was going to blackmail me with all his robbing and such.

No such luck, though. I would have liked to have seen him again, and I figure a little of his mud would have just slid right off me.

So it's just me now, what with everybody dead or moved away, and Seth in the hospital. I always figured to send this to the grandkids one day, but now it's great-grandkids, and they're too young for my babble. I guess I'll just put it up in the closet and let it sit there until I die. Then let somebody else figure out what to do with it.

That's the ticket.

Maybe my granddaughter Sherry will know what to do. I like her the best, anyhow. Maybe she'll give it to her kids.

THE LEGENDARY KID DONOVAN

E.K. RECKNOR

Orphaned and far from the
comforts of "civilized" New York, Horace Tate
Pemberton Smith arrives in Tonto's Wickiup,
Arizona, to meet his uncle and ends up
inheriting a bordello. But the trouble really
starts when he gets credit for killing a
renowned gunfighter—and an unwanted
reputation as the baddest man in the land.

0-451-21632-6

Available wherever books are sold or
at penguin.com

GRITTY HISTORICAL ACTION FROM

USA TODAY BESTSELLING

AUTHOR

RALPH
COTTON

Praise for E. K. Recknor

"Spur Award winner Recknor offers a daffy, highly original Western." —*Publishers Weekly*

VENGEANCE TRAIL

I guess it was because we were brothers that they all knew I wanted to see Spats Lannigan dead. Maybe they wanted it as bad as I did. In any case, it was as if we had all signed a document, legal and binding, to trail him to the end.

It was funny, because if you'd asked me six months ago what I wanted with Spats Lannigan, I would have said, "Nothing." He had killed my daddy, but I had decided to let bygones be bygones. But it seemed that, somewhere along the line, I had reversed my position on that topic. I wanted to see this Lannigan for myself, wanted to see him bleed.

I wanted to see him die.

I was going to avenge my daddy, by God, and nothing was going to stop me—least of all my brothers, who were practically leading me to him. I guessed that they wanted some revenge, too, and just figured to let me take care of it for them.

It was all the same to me.